MAGGIE'S MAN

MAGGIE'S MAN

•

JOYCE MARLOW

AVALON BOOKS
THOMAS BOUREGY AND COMPANY, INC.
401 LAFAYETTE STREET
NEW YORK, NEW YORK 10003

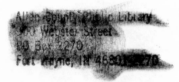

PRINTED IN THE UNITED STATES OF AMERICA
ON ACID-FREE PAPER
BY HADDON CRAFTSMEN, SCRANTON, PENNSYLVANIA

MAGGIE'S MAN

Chapter One

The rushing rapids echoed like thunder through the canyon, a loud, ominous warning of the risky white water just ahead. Maggie Macguire eyed the four people in her raft and hoped they would all make it through safely. No dumps. No swimmers. Just a fast, exciting, roller coaster ride down the Auburn River. That's what Rapid Shooters promised its customers, and that's what she intended to deliver.

Luckily two of her customers today were experienced rafters. Having seasoned hands along always made a run easier and more fun. Gary was the more quiet of the two, while Mark radiated enthusiasm and energy. Standing about six foot two, he had wide shoulders, muscled arms, and a smile that split his rugged face every time he looked her way.

The other two rafters, Heather and Brian Addison, had run the American River last month. Compared to the frenzied ride they would have on the Auburn, the American was as tame as a child's wading pool. She turned around to check on Carl, her father's friend for twenty years and the best guide around. He was piloting the raft that followed fifty feet behind.

Leave it to Carl, she thought, a grin tugging at the corners of her mouth. He was shouting instructions to his crew, drilling them on left and right maneuvers instead of encouraging them to enroll in the week-long training session in guides' techniques that she offered in July. *Another few hundred bucks down the drain,* she thought grimly, then returned her attention to the river.

Quickly facing front, she smiled gamely and told her crew, "Up ahead. First set of Class IVs." A mix of "all rights" and openmouthed silence greeted her. The rapids were a high difficulty rating, and she expected Heather and Brian's pulse rates were soaring into the stratosphere.

"We're going in," she shouted, the hot surge of adrenaline rushing through her veins like wildfire. "Forward! Hard!" She gave instructions to her crew as fast as they could respond, then anchored her feet in the foot cups on the bottom of the canary-colored raft. She tensed her legs and dug her paddle deep into the quickening river.

The other rafters followed her lead, lengthening their strokes to match hers.

"Let's do it!" Mark shouted, his shoulder muscles bulging as he leaned into the stroke. Glancing around, he gave Maggie a roguish hundred-watt smile followed by an exaggerated wink.

She grinned back, then laughed. They'd only met a few hours ago, but he already knew how to make her smile.

They dug into the foaming waves once, twice, and the raft charged into the chute that ran between a line of house-size boulders. Crashing into foaming, whitecapped water, they bucked in the air before slipping into the waves again. A spray of cold water hit the raft full force and streamed down their faces.

Heather gasped aloud and blinked to clear her vision. Maggie noticed that she was struggling to keep up the pace set by the more experienced rafters. Keeping an eye on Heather while maintaining control of the raft, Maggie leaned sharply to the left and dug her paddle into the current. "Now," she urged. "Forward!"

Five paddles dug furiously into the water and the raft plummeted headlong into a series of rapids that cut a rocky path through the boiling current. A split second later they careened close to some giant boulders that emerged on the right.

"Left turn," Maggie ordered, her shoulders

straining to maintain a semblance of control against the fast-moving current. "Left," she urged over the noise of the water. "Harder!"

Grimaces creased their faces as the crew forced the raft away from disaster. Plummeting downstream, they bucked through the chute. The self-bailing raft dipped into a deep hole and flew in the air, causing a torrent of water to blast over them. Half submerged in the raging river, they slipped downstream through continuous rapids, then shot into a large pool of calm water and slid to a stop.

"Yeah!" Mark shouted, water dripping from his face. "What a ride!" He punched the air repeatedly with one clenched fist, rocking the raft up and down, then chanced a look at Maggie. He'd expected to enjoy the run, but he hadn't expected the guide to be so pretty and a redhead to boot.

She had an almost perfect face, with a turned-up nose lightly dusted with golden freckles and eyes the color of exquisite, pale sapphires. The only defect he saw was a slightly crooked front tooth that gave her a whimsical, devil-may-care appearance. Her square jaw hinted at a stubborn streak and he suspected there was a wild side to her. Tame, sedate women didn't run rapids for a living.

"Did you see those gigantic boulders?"

Heather gasped in disbelief. "I thought we were goners."

"No way, honey," Brian assured his wife with a wide grin. "We were under control—barely." Turning to Maggie, who was stuck like glue to the slick, squeaky-wet raft, he grinned even wider and gave her a thumbs-up.

Running one hand through her wet hair, Maggie tucked the long strands behind her ears. Nodding at Brian, she relaxed her leg muscles, and eased her grip on the paddle. Flexing the fingers of one hand, she leaned back and took a long, deep breath. Taking a raft through Class IV rapids was exhilarating, but she never forgot the danger and was glad they'd made it through safely.

"Now I see why they call it Satan's Chute," Heather said to Brian in a shaky voice, then turned around to peer at Maggie. "Who named it that, anyway?"

A deep chuckle rose in Maggie's throat and she cocked one hand against her hip. "My father," she answered proudly. "He was one of the first to run the Auburn more than thirty years ago." An image of her father standing tall and proud, a crooked Irish smile stretched across his heavily whiskered face, sprang into her mind. He was strong and firm, but at the same time fiercely supportive of his children. His death last year had hit hard.

Mark shot her a quizzical look. "Your dad named Satan's Chute?"

"That's right."

"Did he have a nickname?"

"Sure did," Maggie answered smugly. "Red Beard."

Mark cast her an incredulous look. "Your dad had quite a reputation." His dark eyes widened, then he chuckled. "Both in size and story."

"What do you mean?" Heather asked.

Mark glanced at Maggie. "Let me know if I get anything wrong, but Red Beard cut quite a figure. A big man—maybe six foot six—a bushy beard, and a long-handled mustache to match."

"That's right," she confirmed, then added, "waxed into curlicues at both ends."

"And he was one of the first men to commercialize white water rafting," Mark pointed out. "Maggie's father was an environmentalist almost before the word was coined. He helped get laws passed to protect the wilderness areas of the Gold Country, especially the Auburn." He gave Maggie a searching look. "Your father's reputation would be hard to match."

She smiled in agreement. "Did you know him?"

"No, I never got the chance, but anyone who rafts white water has heard of Red Beard. Didn't he hold the first permit on the Auburn?"

"That's right." It felt good to hear someone talk about her father, to know that people in northern California remembered him. She swiveled around to study the foaming rapids they'd just come through. A bright orange raft was about to enter the chute.

"We'd better get moving. Carl's about to hit it." They dipped their paddles into the river, stroking the water in smooth, fluid movements until the raft moved into the current and downstream. After traveling a hundred yards or so, Maggie rested her paddle against the side of the raft.

"Hold steady a minute," she said. "I want to make sure they make it." Craning their necks, everyone watched the raft maneuver the difficult course, bobbing up and down in the current as it picked up speed.

They heard loud shouts above the noise of the roaring current as Carl's raft flew down the chute, luminous blue waves drenching the vessel every few seconds. The raft shot through the long series of rapids, then exploded into the pool they had just left. As if on cue, five paddles simultaneously punched the air and exuberant voices roared above the thunder of the rapids.

"They had a great ride!" Mark almost shouted, giving Maggie a high five. He threaded one hand through thick dark-brown hair that gleamed with tiny beads of water and tilted his face into the sun. Little crinkles appeared at the corners of his eyes as a relaxed expression settled over his face. "I'd love to spend more time here. It's so peaceful." He breathed in the clear mountain air, his chest rising and falling contentedly.

Maggie watched him scan the high golden cliff that ran along one side of the river, then said, "That slice of colored strata about sixty feet up is where the river flowed a thousand years ago, before the water carved out this canyon."

Mark pursed his lips. "Must have been one massive torrent." He shaded his eyes and searched the cloudless blue sky. "I wonder if we'll see any eagles?"

Heather stared up doubtfully. "Eagles?"

"Sure," Mark confirmed. "Golden eagles, hawks . . . this is their home. The human race is just sharing it."

Maggie's eyebrows raised a notch.

"I just wish we'd treat our home with the same respect as its other inhabitants," he added dryly.

Her eyebrows arched even higher. Maybe there was more to Mark Wilde than just hard muscles and a handsome face. Frowning at the thoughts that had come unheeded, she decided she wasn't being very kind—judging people by their looks wasn't a particularly admirable trait. It was just that Mark was so good-looking, so she presumed something had to be wrong with him.

Her father had always preached that handsome men tended to be scoundrels, skirt-chasers, and overly fond of a pint of ale. Although she didn't like to think about it, her own experience had proved him right. She shook her head irritably and blinked, trying to rid herself of the past. It was something she'd been attempting to do for two years, with only limited success.

"There's a feeling about this canyon that's almost spiritual," Mark said, his eyes taking on a faraway look as he turned toward Maggie. "Do you ever get that feeling?"

She leaned against the back of the raft and swallowed hard. Not only did she and Mark seem to have things in common, but she was attracted to him. She hadn't expected that, but maybe she shouldn't be surprised—it had been two years since her breakup with Todd. She'd spent those years in the Peace Corps, living in a remote village in the Philippines. She'd wanted time away from home to think about life and where it was taking her, and the Peace Corps had given her that opportunity.

She'd surprised everyone with the announcement at her college graduation party. Her family had expected to toast her engagement to Todd Whitmore, the handsome blond football star she'd fallen in love with her senior year. But they didn't know that two days after Todd's proposal, Maggie had shown up unexpectedly at his apartment. She'd discovered him with a cute brunette clad in his pajama top—and nothing else.

At first she'd been heartbroken, but after Todd continued to profess his love, a sharp-edged anger hardened like steel around her heart. She could have forgiven him for falling in love with another woman. But it was the dishonesty and deceit that she couldn't forget. Todd had never understood her fury.

Her father had begun a campaign to keep her from shoveling every man into the pit Todd had dug for her. Dad didn't let a day go by without mentioning her mother or repeating some silly anecdote about how he'd courted Mom until she'd finally given in and married him. Maggie had seen her father's love for her mother mirrored in his eyes, and she kept alive a small, secret hope that someday she'd find that special love her parents had shared.

After the breakup with Todd, Maggie decided to do something important with her life that would take her far from home. Teaching English to forty boisterous village children had given her a sense of purpose. The villagers took her into their simple huts and became her friends. In the end, they became the teachers and she the willing student.

They had taught her the kinds of lessons that lasted a lifetime. Honesty, faith, hard work . . . truth.

"Maggie?"

She heard her name and shook the cobwebs free. "Yes," she stammered, taking a deep breath and exhaling slowly. Suddenly she realized she'd been asked a question and hadn't answered.

"I was asking how you felt about the canyon." Mark regarded her for a long moment.

"It's peaceful," she said. "Almost like floating in a time warp. I forget about the outside world when I'm on this stretch of water."

A slight smile settled over Mark's features as he nodded in agreement, then turned to study the tall forest edging the riverbank. "I can see why it could have that effect. Pine, oak, sycamore. The quiet. It's man's country."

"And woman's," Maggie retorted sharply.

He turned back around, gave her an apologetic smile, then laughed out loud. "I stand corrected."

"I should hope so," she replied coolly. The one thing she didn't need on a run was a chauvinistic male. Her experience told her that type usually chose an inopportune time to question either her ability or her authority, and teamwork was essential if they were to get down the river safely.

Mark put out both hands in front of him. "Just

a slip of the tongue," he said with a laugh. "It won't happen again."

Maggie clamped her lips shut. She knew when she was being teased, and she knew when to let a man have the last word. She'd learned that from the village elders. Although she'd managed to get her way when it was important, she'd also learned to let the men think they'd made the decision. It was an age-old female trick that still worked.

"I'm starving," Brian announced. "When's lunch?"

Checking her waterproof watch, Maggie saw it was almost eleven-thirty. She was behind schedule. "We'd better get going. Food is another three miles downriver, but we've got to get through a stretch of slow Class II water, and that means a lot of paddling. Should take about an hour."

"You know, your dad's almost a legend at the BLM," Mark told her.

"The BLM?" she repeated in a tight voice.

"Bureau of Land Management."

"I know what the BLM is," she said uneasily. "What do you have to do with the bureau?"

"Gary and I are planners."

A slight frown creased Maggie's forehead.

"But when summer hits, we patrol the rivers."

Her frown deepened. "I thought only rangers had that authority. Isn't it their job to look things over?" She sucked on her bottom lip and reminded herself that the bureau had said they'd give her some time. They'd as much as promised.

"That's right." Mark nodded. "But the budget doesn't cover salaries for all the rangers we need in the summer, so they reassign a few of us shirt-and-ties. We get to spend the summer, or part of it anyway, as temporary rangers. It's the best part of working for the government." He smiled brightly. "Out-in-the-sun, wind-in-your-face, shoot-the-rapids fringe benefits."

Maggie drew her brows down, swallowed hard, and cleared her throat. "Are you here for a surprise check?"

"Nah," Mark assured her. "But I'll put in for Rapid Shooters when it comes up. You'll be an easy inspection."

Maggie wondered whether she should believe him. It was quite a coincidence, but if he was telling the truth, it was a small reprieve. Very small, but it just might be enough to get the job done. But could she carry out her plan with two BLM employees around? Not that she was doing anything wrong—just the opposite. But if word leaked out that Rapid Shooters was being investigated by the bureau, she might as well pack it in. Nobody put their trust in a company that was under a cloud of suspicion, especially not paying customers.

"What do you check for?" Brian asked Mark.

"That bureau rules and regulations are followed, that the guides know safety measures inside and out, and that they're experts when it comes to rapids. The outfitters have to take certain environmental precautions too."

"You're kidding." Brian stared openmouthed. "How could someone damage the environment by rafting?"

"Easy," Mark answered. "Shrubs and ground cover can be ruined by dragging rafts out of the put-in area instead of carrying them. You have lunch on a full-day run and that means trash and garbage. You can't just leave it. Right, Maggie?"

"Uh-huh," she muttered, averting her eyes to watch the river. She had the feeling that he was issuing her a warning, and the conversation was hitting too close to home. Mark was either very clever, or it really was a coincidence that he and Gary were on the run. What was the truth?

"Remember last summer?" Mark nodded to Gary. "When that new guy with River Runners decided to have a smoke after lunch and tossed a match into the brush? The idiot went on downriver. Didn't even know a fire had started to smolder. What a day *that* was."

Gary shook his head solemnly. "One I hope never to repeat."

"Luckily another outfitter saw the fire before

it spread," Mark explained. "He and his crew put out the flames, then reported it."

"What did you do?" Brian asked.

"Cited the outfitter. One more foul-up and he'll lose his permit."

"But how did you know who caused the fire? Couldn't it have been a camper?"

"No," Mark answered. "The outfitters all have designated put-in areas. Besides, everybody knows everybody around here. It just took a little legwork to figure out who was responsible."

Maggie ran one hand through her wet tangles and took a deep, steadying breath. She couldn't tell if he was talking hypothetically or hinting at her own problems. Whichever it was, she wanted to change the subject. Scanning the river, she saw a stretch of white water coming up. That would draw their attention.

"Rapids up ahead!" she called out.

Brian shaded his eyes and scanned the river. "Any rough ones?"

"No," she assured him. "We don't hit Maytag until after lunch."

"Maytag? What's that?" he asked.

Mark answered before Maggie had a chance. "A Class IV rapids, and better than Satan's Chute."

"You're right there," she agreed heartily. "The formation's named after a washing machine.

Halfway through the rapid there's an eight-foot drop, then we hit a flat spot, paddle like heck to get out before the water spins us around like a load of dirty laundry, shoot down another drop, and then hit another stretch of IV rapids.''

"Oh," Heather said softly. "Sounds like fun."

Mark and Gary both threw back their heads and laughed.

"Ignore these guys," Maggie reassured her. "You'll do fine. But right now we're going into a couple of miles of frisky rapids followed by some quiet, smooth stretches."

Scanning the banks of the river every chance she got, Maggie watched for changes in the terrain, signs of erosion, and other evidence that Patrick and Carl had warned her about. A lot had happened on the river in the last six months, and it had all been bad for Rapid Shooters. Assuming nothing interfered with her plan, she would make some headway today.

She looked behind her. Carl had closed the distance between the rafts during the last mile and was only about forty feet behind them. His crew consisted of a married couple in their midforties and their three teenage sons, all about the same size, clean-cut and blond. Maggie had a hard time remembering who was who, especially since their parents had named them Bill, Brady, and Brett.

She cupped one hand to her mouth and shouted, "How'd you like Satan's Chute?"

"It was a blast," one of the teenagers yelled back.

"I thought we were gonna bag it," another exclaimed with a wide grin.

Carl dismissed the thought by waving one burly hand. "Piece of cake. Got the makings of some darn good rafters in these boys here," he declared. "I'll take 'em downriver anytime."

All three teenagers beamed and their parents laughed. One of the boys slapped Carl on the back. "Thanks, Pops. We just might take you up on that."

"We're porting at that clearing up ahead," Maggie announced.

Gary rolled his eyes and patted his stomach. "I hope that means lunch."

"It does," she assured him. "Let's go."

A few minutes later, she jumped into the goosebump–cold, thigh-high water as they veered close to the riverbank. Mark quickly followed her, and together they pulled the rafts over the hard-packed mud by the lead ropes, holding fast while everyone clambered out. Mark took the line from Maggie and anchored it around a sturdy bush. He secured the other raft by tying the lead around a large boulder and knotting the rope several times.

Maggie glanced at the table set up in the small

clearing a few feet away. Their driver had set out huge rolls, deli meats, cheeses, and bowls of hard-boiled eggs, potato salad and coleslaw. Plates, utensils, and napkins rested on boulders nearby. Everyone milled around the table, hungry enough to eat anything that moved.

"Help yourselves," she said to the group, then noticed that Mark seemed to be standing back. Was he waiting for her?

He stretched his arms overhead, then folded them across his chest. "It's been a great day. Fast white water and a great bunch of people. What more could you ask for?"

"Not much," she agreed. "That's why I enjoy my business so much. It's great."

He glanced down at her. "Do you live close by, or just commute when you have a run?"

"Commute?" She jerked her head back. "You couldn't get me to commute, and you couldn't tear me away from the Auburn, or my home, for very long," she said staunchly. "I live in the house where I was born."

"That's unusual these days. What town?"

"Sycamore Springs."

"Nice place. I've been through there on my way to go fishing. So you're one of those old-fashioned small-town girls, right?"

Maggie rolled her eyes. "Hardly. In fact, I consider myself just the opposite." Hearing raised voices, she glanced toward the table. The sounds of laughter and good-natured ribbing by the brothers punctuated the silence of the pristine canyon.

"You better grab some food before it's all gone," she suggested, noticing the teenagers had huge sandwiches in both hands and the others were fixing smaller versions.

"Good idea," he said. "I'm starved. How about you?"

"I'll be there in a minute. You go ahead."

"Join me," Mark pressed. "I promise I won't bite."

Maggie took a deep breath and swallowed hard. She had work to do and was running out of time. She'd have to ignore the sounds rumbling through her empty stomach. "I'll be over in a minute," she promised, knowing full well she wouldn't.

Chapter Two

"**I**'ll save you a spot," he said, wondering if Maggie would join him or if she was just being polite. He wanted to get to know her better, but she seemed deliberately uninterested. An unsettling thought crossed his mind. Maybe she was involved with someone. He hadn't met a woman who piqued his interest in a long time, and it would be just his luck if she was already taken.

A grim shadow stole over his face as he assembled two huge sandwiches and heaped coleslaw on his plate. He hoped his position at the BLM wasn't the problem. He knew mixing business with pleasure wasn't a good idea. In fact, it was impossible. He glanced up at the clear blue sky and brightened. Just because she held a commercial rafting permit didn't mean there was an inherent conflict. As usual, when it came to his job, he was being overly cautious.

The minute Mark turned his back, Maggie walked toward the orange raft where Carl sat hunched over, fiddling with the fastenings on a life jacket. He'd been her dad's friend for twenty years and godfather to both her and Patrick, her brother. She trusted Carl with her life. When her dad died last year, he'd been the one to telephone. She could still hear Carl's low, gruff voice, choked with emotion, explaining how Dad had been chopping wood when the heart attack struck. Carl had found him a few minutes later. A few minutes too late.

He glanced up as she approached, a scowl on his rough, weather-beaten face. "We'd better attend to these spare jackets, missy. That's four with broken ties." He frowned, then peered closely at the jacket again. "I don't understand it. I went over all the equipment three weeks back."

"Maybe you missed a few," she suggested, adding the task of inspecting the equipment to her weekly work list.

Carl's frown deepened. "Maybe I'm getting old," he said in a resigned voice.

Maggie swallowed hard. Since she'd been back, she'd noticed Carl seemed forgetful. He was slowing down, and as much as she hated to think about it, she knew the time was coming when he couldn't raft white water. But how could she tell him without making it sound as if he were being put out to pasture? She decided to discuss it with Patrick the first chance she got.

"What's up?" Carl asked. "You look like you've lost your best friend."

She took in the tanned, wrinkled lines of his face and remembered his best friend—her father. Dad would have hated to be told he couldn't live up to his rafting reputation any longer. They'd figure out other things for Carl to do, something to show that he was still valuable to their operation. But now wasn't the time to bring it up. Instead, she said, "The two guys on my raft, Mark and Gary. . . . "

Carl stood up, a wide smile spreading over his face. "Don't tell me you've got something against the tall one who's been hankering after you all morning."

She frowned. "I'd hardly call it that, Carl."

"Hah! Then you don't know your men, missy."

Maggie ignored the comment, put one hand on Carl's shoulder, and leaned close. Her voice softened to a hushed whisper. "They're with the BLM."

"What, already? That letter, the directive, came what—two weeks ago?"

"Just about," Maggie confirmed.

He gave her a hard look. "It must be a coincidence. They promised you more time, and it's too soon to send investigators. Besides, those two are having too much fun to be working.'' He stuck both hands in his pockets. ''What's got you so spooked? We've still got plenty of time to make things right.''

Maggie let out a big breath, then rubbed her temple where she felt a headache start to pulse. She'd only been back in the States for two weeks, and she already had more trouble than she knew how to handle. Suddenly her little jungle village seemed like paradise lost and her home a morass of modern problems.

''I had hoped to comply with the directive before everybody found out about this mess. What little business we have left could disappear like that''—she snapped her fingers—''if word gets out.''

She nodded toward the rafters, who were happily eating lunch and talking among themselves. ''I'm going ahead as planned. Once they realize I'm gone, just say I went for a hike. That'll give me enough time to get the job done. When I come back, I'll circle around and put everything in the bus. Then I won't have to answer any questions.''

''Maggie, why don't you stay here? I can—''

She shook her head emphatically. ''I was up there just last week. I know exactly where the site is.'' *And,* she told herself, *I move faster than you do.*

Carl rubbed a hand across the back of his neck. "All right. I know better than to try and change your mind once it's made up. You're just like your dad—stubborn as a mule." He leaned down into the raft, opened the waterproof dry bag secured under the lip, retrieved a heavy green plastic bag, and handed it to her. "Be careful," he warned.

Maggie's lips were set in a tight line. She had a job to do and nothing was going to stop her. There was too much at stake. "Just keep them occupied. Tell some old rafting stories. Anything."

"Okay, missy. That I can do."

Maggie carried the bag close to her chest as she walked along the riverbank, then turned inland fifty feet downstream toward a stand of sycamores and pines. The trees were greener than she'd ever seen. The spring rains had plumped the leaves and branches full of new life. She breathed in the clean smell of the earth as she threaded her way along the rocky terrain, quickly entered the forest, and disappeared from view. Her determined footsteps were muffled by the dry pine needles that covered the ground like a blanket.

Ten minutes later, she walked up a slight incline and stepped into a twenty-foot-wide clearing ringed by majestic California redwoods towering toward the sky. Their pine-scented branches created a lacy curtain of green that reflected the heat of the midday sun, leaving the area cool and inviting. But the beautiful foliage couldn't hide what was scattered beneath the trees.

Trash. Everywhere. Crumpled napkins, plates, cups, and plastic bags were tossed on the ground. Garbage, cigarette packs, and matchbooks had been thrown into a crudely made fire pit and partially burned. She picked up a matchbook and read the cover. It was the Dew Drop Inn, a bar near the edge of town. If she remembered correctly, it had a seedy reputation. She bent down, retrieved a red-and-white cigarette pack from where it lay crumpled on the ground, and slipped them both in her back pocket.

Angry furrows creased her brow. Spying what appeared to be a paddle half hidden under a fallen tree branch, she walked over and knelt down on the ground to examine it. The distinctive neon-yellow initials of Rapid Shooters were emblazoned on one side. The paddle was broken in two, and the edges of one piece were burned. It looked as if someone had tried to get rid of the evidence, but had only partially succeeded.

''Jake Rawnick,'' she mumbled with contempt, knowing all he'd done—lying, cheating, and worse. When Patrick hired him, all his paperwork had been in order, or so it seemed. Although his CPR certificate had been legitimate, the glowing letter of recommendation from an outfitter in Colorado had been forged. When Patrick called to check the reference, he discovered that the owner had sold the business and gone on a month long rafting expedition to New Zealand. The new owner didn't know Rawnick, and he couldn't find any personnel files.

Patrick had been doing the work of two people for the last four months, and he was up against the wall. He had to hire a guide right away. Married less than a year, with a wife who was eight months pregnant, he'd been working twelve-hour days, operating both the store and the rafting business singlehandedly. He hired Rawnick, then marked his calendar to call the supposed reference when he returned from New Zealand.

By then it was too late. The damage had been done, and now Maggie and Patrick faced the possibility of losing the permit their father had held for thirty years and passed on to them when he died. Although they'd worked out a plan to save the business, she wondered if they could pull it off.

As upset as she was over her predicament, Maggie was more concerned about the havoc Rawnick had wreaked on her cherished Auburn River wilderness. She surveyed the clearing, shaking her head at the dozens of seedlings, only six or seven inches high, that had been trampled and killed.

So many had been destroyed, it appeared to have been done on purpose.

Opening the plastic bag, she took out a miniature trowel, a dozen tiny seedlings wrapped in damp paper, and a gallon jug of water. Digging out each lifeless tree with the trowel, she dropped them in the bag, planted new seedlings in their place, and tenderly covered the roots with earth before watering each one.

Putting the trowel in her back pocket, Maggie wiped her hands on her shorts before walking around the clearing and stuffing trash into the bag. She scanned the ground for any small bits of paper she might have missed, finally deciding the clearing appeared natural, the way it had before Rawnick had come out of nowhere and ruined everything.

Grabbing the bag of trash in one hand and cradling the pieces of broken paddle in the other, she started down the path and almost immediately caught sight of a tall man with a long-legged, purposeful stride coming toward her through the trees. She squinted her eyes and slowed her pace, trying to figure out who it was. She stopped dead in her tracks, her breath caught in her lungs. She ran her tongue over her mouth, swallowed hard, and forced her mouth into a semblance of a smile.

''Mark—what are you doing here?'' she asked anxiously when he was a dozen feet away.

He quickly closed the distance between them. "I was getting worried. Carl said you went hiking, but you were gone a long time." He glanced at the heavy bag she carried. "What's that?"

Maggie bit down on her lower lip. "Just some trash," she said, not daring to meet his eyes. "I found a lot of litter scattered around, and I always carry a bag with me. . . . " She trembled as her voice trailed off in a hopeless lie.

She glanced up, sideways, anyplace but directly at Mark. She hated inventing stories. Nervously running her tongue over her bottom lip, she remembered that when she was little, her father always knew when she was fibbing by the guilty look in her eyes. "You know how careless some people are," she finished lamely.

"I'll say. Let me have that." Mark reached out his hand.

"No," she objected, tightening her grip.

Laughing, he pulled hard and took it from her. "C'mon. Let me be a gentleman."

She watched the heavy bag swing from her grip to his, hoping it wouldn't spill open. When it didn't she felt a wave of relief wash over her.

He nodded at what she held in the other hand. "How about that?"

She glanced down. "I've got it," she insisted, holding the pieces of paddle inward to hide the bright yellow letters. She couldn't admit it belonged to her company. If he started asking questions, she would have to conjure up a bigger lie.

"So, Maggie, what do you do with yourself when you're not leading expeditions down the Auburn?" Mark asked as they started down the trail.

"We have a store in town called Outdoor Odyssey. It's mainly backpacking supplies and outdoor gear—"

"We?" he repeated the word hesitantly.

She gave him a blank look. "My brother and I."

Relief flashed across his tanned face. "You're in business with your brother? Good!"

Maggie glanced back, confused. Mark had an odd way of asking questions. "Not that my brother and I don't have our differences on how to run things."

"Well, that's to be expected," he said. "But somehow I can't see you working behind a counter."

"You're right. I hate it. I've been trying to figure out a way for Patrick to manage without me, but it takes two people, and we can't afford to hire anyone right now. How do you like working for the BLM?" she asked, not caring, but wanting to change the subject.

"It's okay. The work's satisfying once you get past the bureaucracy. I'm involved with the California Rivers Coalition, so Sacramento is a good place to be.''

''I've heard of the coalition,'' she said. ''In the last few weeks, I've read a couple of articles about their environmental work. Aren't they opposing that dam the government wants to build?''

''Absolutely. That's why my boss doesn't appreciate my involvement.''

''I can understand why. Isn't it a federal project?''

''Yep,'' he said, tight-lipped. ''And if it's built on the Auburn, all this will be underwater.''

She glanced around at the untouched natural beauty of the wilderness, the trees that almost hugged the sky, the incredibly clear river that roared fast and free down the canyon, and the forest animals that scurried unseen through the underbrush.

''I'd hate to see that happen,'' she said glumly, falling silent. Patrick had told her all about the plan to build a massive hydroelectric dam on the Auburn. When she looked around, she knew the cost was too high. Some things couldn't be measured by the almighty dollar.

''The director considers my work a conflict of interest, but I disagree. The BLM protects the rivers and the coalition has the same goals. I don't see a conflict.''

She angled him a wry smile. "I hope you don't need your paycheck to buy groceries."

He threw back his head and laughed. "I sure do, but I hope it won't come to that. It would be a tough choice."

She glanced sideways at him again, noticing the seriousness of his expression. The coalition was an important environmental group committed to protecting endangered wildlife and forested areas. It looked as if she and Mark had more in common than white water rafting.

"I have some literature on the dam," she said. "It came to the store last week."

"You're probably on our mailing list. The coalition sends monthly fliers to every outfitter in the state. Why don't you get involved? We could use the help."

"I do have a stake in whatever happens on the Auburn. My father would turn over in his grave if he thought the river was threatened and I hadn't tried to stop it."

"Why don't I call you next week?" he suggested as they walked into the put-in area. "We're having a meeting on Tuesday night. You can find out more about the coalition and I'll introduce you around."

Maggie thought about what Mark had said. If she was home to stay, she had to get involved. "All right," she said. "I'll make the time."

Noticing a dozen eyes aimed in their direction and realizing she'd been gone longer than planned, Maggie decided to say something. "Carl, how's lunch coming?"

"Just finished a few minutes ago. Ready to head on out."

Turning back to Mark, she asked, "What time's the meeting?"

"We start at seven and go for a couple of hours."

She pursed her lips thoughtfully. "There's a possibility that I may have to back out at the last minute. My sister-in-law is due to have a baby any day now, and—"

Carl approached them and nodded toward the bus that waited a dozen yards away. "How about if I take that," he said tersely, pointing to the plastic bag Mark held. "The driver's ready to go."

"No problem. I'll do it, Carl," Mark insisted.

Maggie breathed a bit easier as she walked over to the raft and deposited the pieces of broken oar. What was it her father had said about liars always getting caught? She already felt guilty and she hadn't done anything wrong, except tell a few white lies. She bit down on her lower lip and felt guilt surround her like a heavy cloak. Who was she kidding? White lies, black lies. They were all the same. Dishonesty was wrong under any circumstances.

She glanced around and frowned at the questioning looks she saw on the other rafters' faces. Brett, Brady, and Bill had their heads together, whispering. Each wore a silly grin. She wondered what was so funny. Why were they acting so secretive?

When one of them gave Mark a thumbs-up and a broad wink as he walked toward the raft, she realized what they were thinking—that she and Mark had been off on a romantic romp in the woods. Terrific. She rolled her eyes. *That's all I need.*

"Let's get going," she said with tight lips, deciding she couldn't do much about what the boys were thinking other than to get on with the business at hand.

"You didn't have lunch," Mark protested. "You must be hungry."

"I never eat lunch on a run," she muttered, ignoring the growling noises coming from her stomach. She had a healthy appetite and usually ate more than her share, but not today. There wasn't time. She glanced at her watch. Two o'clock. Her cleanup operation had put them off schedule. She perched her hands on her hips and surveyed the group as they ambled to the rafts and clambered in.

"Make sure your jackets are secured," she reminded them. "We'll switch off for the afternoon and let Carl take the lead."

An hour later, they heard the rapids. Even from a distance, the sound of boiling, churning water resounded through the still air. Maggie cupped her hands to her mouth and yelled Carl's name over the noise of crashing waves. When he turned and looked back, she raised her hand, motioned toward the riverbank, and yelled, "Let's pull up."

Following Carl, she guided her raft to one side and into a relatively calm pool of water edged by a large boulder garden and waist-high reeds. Anchoring her paddle between two large rocks, she stabilized the raft.

"Okay. Listen up." Maggie raised her voice so everyone could hear. "This is the best part of the trip, what most of you came for: Maytag—a Class IV cataract that's challenging and very dangerous."

"What's a cataract?" someone asked hesitantly.

"A waterfall," she answered.

Heather gasped. "We're going down a waterfall?"

"No." Maggie shook her head, holding up two fingers. "We're going down two. Maytag and a second small fall. Son of Maytag. The first's an eight-foot torrent that we hit hard. Then we drop down to a large, flat area.''

She searched their faces for signs of fear. Being nervous was a healthy sign; she didn't want any instant heroes. But if someone was truly afraid, she'd give them the option of hiking out. Satisfied that they were primed and ready to go for it, she went on.

"Watch closely—please. This is crucial if we're to get over the falls safely. Just before the raft goes over the falls, pull your paddles in and duck down like this.'' Maggie crouched down in the raft and bent her head into her chest while holding the paddle tightly under both arms.

She angled her head up and continued. "After two or three seconds, I'll yell 'up.' Then get back in position, dig your paddles in the water, and give it some muscle. We'll go full-out. Any questions?'' She waited, scanning each face.

Mark studied her closely. "Why don't we paddle through it?'' he asked. "If there's trouble, we need to react immediately. Wouldn't we have more control if we could see what's ahead while running the falls?''

Maggie nodded. "You have some good points, but there's not enough time. We'll be over in less than ten seconds. If we go in right, we'll hit the flat dead-on. The important thing is to jump up and paddle like crazy when we do hit.''

"And if we don't go in right?" Mark asked.

"We will. That's my job," she answered firmly. "It's only a hundred yards to the next drop. You can ride Son of Maytag upright, but bring in your paddles. We don't want a dump. There's another stretch of Class IV rapids a hundred yards down."

Mark's expression turned serious and he nodded.

Good, Maggie mouthed silently. *He trusts my judgment.* She didn't mind his questions; it showed he was paying serious attention to the situation. And he'd listened to what she'd said and accepted it. If he hadn't, it wouldn't have been the first time. She was used to butting heads with macho types who thought they knew more about rafting than she did. It was always awkward, telling them it was her way or no way.

"What's a dump?" Heather asked.

"When a rafter swims the rapids without benefit of the raft." She looked into their faces, sure that they understood what she'd said. "More questions?" Hearing no response, she gave them a reassuring smile. "There's a massive boulder, big as a house, farther downriver that we want to steer around. You'll know we're almost there when I call for a hard left turn. If we aren't careful, we could wrap."

"Okay, coach, what's a wrap?" Brian asked tentatively.

"Getting stuck on the boulder. The pressure of the water doubles the raft and wraps it around the rock. Sometimes it takes a bit of maneuvering to get off. This is what you're here for," she reminded them, raising her voice over the sound of the boiling water. "Remember to listen for the commands and paddle full-out. We don't want to swim Maytag or the stretch of waves, boulders, and holes that comes after."

Carl spoke up. "If you dump, remember to position your feet forward. Otherwise you'll skin yourself up on the rocks. The life jacket will keep your head above water. Try and reach the side of the river, find a rock or a tree branch, and hold on. We'll pick you up."

"Carl will lead." Maggie glanced around, still searching for any signs of hesitancy. All she saw were looks of determination and expectation. "As soon as Carl is through Maytag and headed into the second fall, we'll start."

"Why do we run the rafts so close together?" Gary asked.

"In case we have swimmers," Carl answered calmly.

"Maggie," one of the teenagers piped up. "How many times have you been down Maytag?"

Before she could answer, another brother piped up, "How many times have people dumped?"

Maggie shrugged. There was no point in talking numbers. Over the years, she'd seen hundreds of accidents—and more than a few serious—but those stories wouldn't reassure her team. Instead she said, "There's always a chance of dumping on a Class IV, but I've seen it happen on a smooth Class II. Just remember"—she pointed toward Maytag—"aim your feet downriver and away from the boulders."

"Heck, I could use a swim." Mark smiled broadly.

"Yeah, me too!" Bill agreed.

"Let's go," Carl said, dipping his paddle into the river and taking a deep stroke. "Forward now. Hard!" he yelled to his crew.

"Let's go for it!" Bill shouted.

"All right!" his brothers chimed in.

The bright orange raft jetted downstream toward the boiling current as Maggie and her crew watched, wondering if disaster would hit Carl's raft—or theirs.

"Pull. Twice more," Maggie heard Carl yell as the raft sped over the waves toward Maytag. The water turned rough the closer they came, the waves capping with splashes of white foam. The orange raft slid halfway under the waves, then surfaced with increasing frequency. At times,

Maggie completely lost sight of it for a second or two. Suddenly the raft bobbed up, paddles flew through the water-laced air, and it disappeared.

"They're over!" Maggie shouted. "Let's go!"

Chapter Three

Everyone dug into the river, grabbing the water with their paddles until the raft was propelled into the current.

"Stroke! Stroke!" Maggie called out hoarsely.

White-knuckled hands gripped the paddles, shoulders straining, arms extended, digging deep into the river.

"Pull—again!"

The raft ducked into the white-capped waves, coming ever closer to the drop-off that lay fifty feet ahead, where the foaming torrent of water came to an abrupt halt. Maggie clamped down on her teeth, tensing her legs so hard against the back of the raft that she became an immovable object. It was crucial that she stay with the raft.

"Hold on!" she shouted. "We're going over."

She tensed her legs even tighter. They were within ten feet of the edge. "Paddles up. In the raft!'' she urged as they rushed toward the thundering brink.

When only three people crouched down, paddles curled under their arms, Maggie glanced at Mark. His upright stance signaled his intention to ride the falls with her, coolly staring danger straight in the face. The raft picked up speed and hurtled through the foam-sprayed air in a race toward the falls.

Maggie's eyes were as wide as saucers when the raft plummeted through space to meet the river. She only had a split second to wonder if Mark knew what he was doing; she had no time for a man gambling with heroics. They hit bottom with a lurch, water streaming into the raft from all sides.

Maggie shook her head to clear her vision and saw Heather start to go over the edge. In the same instant Maggie moved toward her, Mark reached out and pulled Heather in. She landed in the middle, unhurt and scrambling for her seat.

''You all right?'' Maggie yelled, retrieving Heather's paddle from the bottom of the raft.

''I th-think so,'' Heather stammered, gulping in air.

Maggie gave Mark a quick look, then plunged her paddle into the foaming water. ''Stroke hard!'' she called to the crew. ''Full-out!'' Water streamed down their faces as the rafters thrust their paddles into the water and dug into the waves.

"Forward—harder!" she yelled again. The next fall was dead ahead. "Son of Maytag, here we come!" A reckless grin spread across her face. She saw from the tight grips on their paddles and the swell of excitement in their voices that her crew was ready. When her eyes met Mark's, her grin widened.

She could tell they shared the anticipation of the challenge to come. This was what she loved, and having someone to share it with made the experience even more thrilling. She reveled in the excitement of being on the cutting edge and meeting danger head-on. The feeling was just as exhilarating the thousandth time as the first.

"Yippee!" Gary shouted.

"Let's do it!" Brian yelled.

Mark felt the adrenaline pump as they edged over the top and fell down in a split second, hitting bottom so hard that he gasped when a deluge of cold water sprayed the raft. It was great. Not as treacherous as Hell's Canyon or Burnt Gorge, but definitely a first-rate ride . . . with a first-rate guide. He wondered if Maggie had ever gone downriver in a kayak. The thought crossed his mind that he would enjoy teaching her.

"Whew," Maggie spluttered, dragging her hair over one shoulder so she could see. Her eyes opened to see Mark staring straight at her, a big smile plastered across his face. Her pulse rate jammed. Suddenly a movement up ahead pulled her attention. A hint of color had flashed across the blue and white of the river.

Mark followed her eyes and half stood in the raft, angling his head to see. Carl's raft had come out of a deep hole. He'd bottomed out. A body was in the river.

"Let's go!" Maggie shouted urgently. "There's a swimmer. He's behind the raft." It looked like one of the boys. He was struggling and flailing his arms wildly.

"Pull right!" Mark told them, tracking the direction the boy was moving in. "I'll get him."

"Right turn!" Maggie urged through gritted teeth.

Everyone pulled against the roaring current, muscles strained to the max, faces contorted with the struggle to reach the boy fighting to stay afloat in the cold torrent of water.

Maggie fervently prayed that he could hold on another minute. They were almost there. She could see his head between the waves, bobbing up and down, frantically trying to stay above water. When they were ten feet from him, Mark threw his paddle into the raft, leaned over the side, and reached both arms deep into the river. Maggie grabbed the paddle. They didn't want to lose it.

Stark fear flashed through her mind. What if Mark went in too?

Mark grabbed the top of the boy's life jacket and held on. He paused for a split-second to tighten his grip, then jerked hard. The boy came halfway out of the water, and Mark pulled again. They both fell backward, collapsing on top of each other in the pool of cold water that had collected in the bottom of the raft.

Bill was numb and cold from shock. His breathing was labored as he gulped air.

"Keep paddling forward," Maggie shouted to the crew, tucking both paddles under one arm. She crouched down on her knees, reached under the lip of the raft for a dry bag, then chanced a look at Mark.

"Get his life jacket off—and his shirt." She stowed the paddles then ripped open the dry bag and pulled out a waterproof thermal jacket while Mark tore at Bill's shirt and jerked it over the boy's head. Water streamed over the sides of the self-bailing raft, soaking Mark and further chilling the boy.

"Bill, are you okay?" Maggie asked. When she got no response, she reached over and shook him. "Bill!"

He nodded through lips blue from the cold. His teeth chattered so loud, the noise could be heard above the rush of the river.

"I did a quick check," Mark told her tightly. "Scrapes on one leg, ankle, and thigh. No serious cuts."

She quickly ran her eyes over the abrasions. They were raw and bleeding, but not profusely. A little first-aid work would take care of them. The important thing was to elevate his body temperature as quickly as possible.

"I'm . . . o-k-kay," Bill chattered. "J-just . . . c-cold."

She handed Mark the tight-fitting thermal shirt. He tugged it over the boy's clammy body, closing the zippers on the sleeve and neck openings. She glanced up, relieved to see a calm stretch of water just ahead and Carl's raft a hundred feet away. She saw him rise, then wave his oar overhead. She grabbed a paddle, held it high, and waved back, a signaling that everything was okay.

"Hey, m-man, I said I w-wanted a swim, d-didn't I?" Bill clattered between his teeth. He turned to Mark, suddenly serious. "Thanks for p-p-ulling me in."

Mark made a small dismissive gesture with one hand.

"How did it happen?" Heather asked.

"I d-d-don't know," Bill muttered, wide-eyed. He dragged a hand over his face to wipe away the water. "We hit the second fall and. . . . " His eyes grew wider. "I went in."

"It's an easy place to dump," Maggie confirmed. "You'd think the smaller fall would be less dangerous, but it's not. I've gone in there a few times myself."

"You . . . have?" Bill asked in a halting voice.

She nodded and stared him straight in the eyes. "It goes with the territory." She took out a foil pack from the dry bag, ripped it open with her teeth, and removed an antiseptic-laden gauze. She swabbed at the cuts on his thigh, ignoring his sharp intake of breath, then moved the gauze to his ankle and pressed hard on the scrape. She could feel him tense as she swabbed his skin.

"Sorry," she whispered, meeting Bill's eyes.

He blinked away the pain and steadied his chin.

A minute later, Maggie leaned against the back of the raft. "You'll be one big ache tomorrow, but otherwise I think you're all right."

Mark gave him a hand up and moved over, giving Bill room to sit next to him.

"All right, guys. Let's go," Maggie said, taking up her position at the rear. "The day isn't over yet." Giving in to the tension, she let out a sigh and felt a wave of relief pass over her. She handled emergencies well, but she always felt like jelly afterward. Thank goodness it was afterward, she reminded herself.

That's why Patrick never took customers on a run. Although he knew the river and was a seasoned rafter, he let anxiety take over during a crisis. And that's why he'd needed help running the business after their father died. With eight months left on her commitment with the Peace Corps, she'd flown home for the funeral, but she'd left again after two weeks. She couldn't have stayed longer.

If she had, the children would have gone into the fields to work and it would have been impossible to get them back. The entire year would have been wasted. That's why Patrick had hired Jake Rawnick in such a hurry. To take her place. She couldn't shake the feeling that if she hadn't gone back to the Philippines, they wouldn't be in this mess. Dad had always counted on her to help with the rafting business and on Patrick to help run the store. She'd failed them both.

Two hours later, the bus rumbled into Sycamore Springs, the brakes screeching loudly as they pulled into the parking lot next to Outdoor Odyssey.

"Thanks for a great run," Gary said, turning to Maggie.

"It was a good day," she agreed, climbing out of the bus.

"Yeah!" Bill, Brady, and Brett chorused as they tumbled down the bus stairs.

Maggie stood beside the bus, laughing as they slapped palms and punched each other as they followed their parents across the parking lot. They were a nice family. The kind she wanted one day. A husband, three or four kids, all out for a day together, just like the hundreds of outings she'd gone on with her parents.

"You take care of those scrapes," she called after Bill.

"No big deal," he insisted staunchly, giving her a friendly wave.

"'Bye," Heather said. "We'll be back."

"Next month," Brian assured her. "I already booked it with Carl."

Maggie cocked her fists against her hips and grinned. Repeat business was always a good sign. Without warning, a hand closed gently over her shoulder. She took a deep breath and slowly turned around, careful not to dislodge the hand she instinctively knew belonged to Mark Wilde. Tilting her head back, she let the air out all at once.

"Hi," he said softly, raising his brows slightly and letting his gaze wander over her face. He'd been watching her all day, and suddenly he realized the day wasn't long enough. He didn't want to leave. Instead, he stood there, trying to think up an excuse to stay.

"Thanks for helping today," she said. "It could have been nasty." She nervously tucked her rumpled T-shirt into her shorts, wondering why she was nervous.

"No problem." He paused, then said casually, "About the coalition meeting on Tuesday. I hope things work out so you can come."

"That's up to Baby Macguire."

"Why don't I give you a call on Tuesday afternoon?"

"All right. I should know one way or the other by then."

"Good. I think you'll enjoy meeting everyone at the coalition." He ran one hand behind his neck. "Uh . . . I don't have your phone number."

"Oh. Sorry." She looked around. "Do you have something to write on?"

He felt his face redden. He was as flustered as a gangly fifteen-year-old asking for his first date. What was the matter with him? "Hold on." He glanced across the parking lot. "I'll be right back."

She watched him amble over to a shiny black Ranger, then followed him across the blacktop. She realized he was whistling and cocked her head to listen, then put one hand over her mouth to suppress a chuckle. It was an Elvis tune she'd heard a hundred times, "Love Me Tender," and Mark was way off key.

He retrieved a pen and a scrap of paper, wrote down the number she gave him, then opened the door and slid in. After he'd started the motor, he leaned out the window, took a chance, and ruffled her hair. "I'll call you on Tuesday."

Maggie swatted at his hand, patted her curls, then watched him pull out of the parking lot. She took a deep breath and swallowed hard. Tuesday was only two days away. Smiling to herself, she walked slowly back across the parking lot and through the front door of the outdoor gear store that doubled as the headquarters of Rapid Shooters. Patrick was getting ready to close when she walked in.

He stood by the cash register, pencil tucked behind one ear, counting the day's receipts. "How'd it go?"

"We had one swimmer with some scrapes and bruises, but nothing serious."

He looked up. "Where'd you dump?"

"Son of Maytag."

Patrick pursed his lips knowingly. "That's the usual place. I've had a few bad spills between the two falls." He retrieved the pencil, wrote some figures on a piece of paper, slipped them into the cash register, and locked it.

"Are you having dinner with us tonight?" he asked, closing the vertical blinds on the large plate-glass window at the front of the shop.

She sighed, then nodded. "I tried to beg off, but Kerry insisted. When is she going to take a rest? She's liable to be baking a pie when my niece comes.''

"Or nephew," Patrick said with a smile. ''You know Kerry. She insists on cooking a hot meal every night. Actually. . . . '' He ran a hand over his brow and closed his eyes for a second. "She's feeling fine. I'm the one who's a wreck.''

Maggie noticed his haggard expression and decided *exhausted* was probably a better word. ''You do look tired. Let's go home and give Kerry a hand.''

They quickly walked the three blocks comprising Sycamore Springs's downtown toward the stately, two-story Victorian house they'd inherited from their parents. Maggie had tried to find separate lodgings when she'd returned, but Kerry and Patrick had insisted that she stay. Their father had left the house to brother and sister in equal shares, and there was plenty of space. Five bedrooms, three baths, and a half-dozen other rooms.

Maggie wondered what she would tell Kerry once they got home. Most people greeted you with, ''Hello, how was your day?'' But not Kerry. Maggie knew her first question would be, ''Did you meet any nice men today?'' Kerry was bound and determined that Maggie should settle down and get married, and the sooner, the better.

Memories flooded over her every time she walked through the front door and saw Dad's oxblood leather chair in the living room, worn from years of use and still bearing the impression of his body. She'd expected Patrick to claim it as his own, but he hadn't. In a way, she was glad. Her father had been both her hero and her best friend. The thought of someone taking his place, even sitting in his chair, seemed unthinkable.

"Kerry, we're home," Patrick called out as they made their way toward the kitchen.

Maggie tilted her head in the air and wrinkled her nose. As usual, the aroma of freshly baked bread wafted through the house.

"Ah, love, there you are." Kerry beamed at Patrick from the kitchen door. Her blond hair was tied in a simple ponytail and she wore a loose white blouse with the words AND BABY MAKES THREE embroidered across the front. "Give us a kiss, now," she said, one hand anchored on her lower back, the other resting on her protruding abdomen.

Maggie decided the young Welsh woman Patrick had met in church one Sunday and married four months later was perfect for her brother. Every time she saw Kerry, she smiled, and every time she watched Patrick and Kerry together, her grin stretched even wider. Their intention to produce a half-dozen offspring made her especially happy.

"Maggie, who went down the river with you

this morning?'' Kerry asked sweetly. ''Any young men you might take a fancy to?''

Maggie thought for a second, then smiled brightly. ''Yes, and I have dates with all three— Mel Gibson, Tom Cruise, and Johnny Depp.''

Kerry put her hand to her mouth and giggled. ''You're pulling my leg again.''

A picture of Mark flashed through her mind. He was just as attractive as any big-screen heart-throb, but she had no intention of telling Kerry. If she did, she'd never hear the end of it.

''Dinner's ready. Both of you sit down,'' Kerry insisted cheerfully.

''Have you done everything already?'' Maggie glanced at the table, set with white linen, china, and crystal.

''Honey, please. . . . '' Patrick steered Kerry to a chair at the table. ''You sit down and rest. We'll bring everything in.''

Maggie hurried toward the kitchen with Patrick close behind. After spooning brussels sprouts into a bowl, she squirted them with lemon and added a dollop of butter before retrieving the salad from the fridge. Patrick gingerly transferred the chicken to a platter and untied the string that Kerry had wound around the bird's legs.

''I tell you, I'm fine,'' Kerry protested loudly from the dining room. ''I'm only having a baby. I'm not sick, you know.''

Patrick paused from scooping dressing out of the chicken and rested the spoon on the counter. "What am I going to do with that woman?" he asked, a worried expression on his face.

Maggie raised her brows. "Cherish her and thank God you swept her off her feet before some other guy found her." She shook her head at Patrick and they both laughed.

After dinner, Maggie washed the dishes while Patrick settled Kerry in the living room. She was rinsing the suds off the last plate when he walked into the kitchen.

"Did everything go according to plan today?" he asked.

She turned off the water, leaned against the counter, and took a deep breath before answering. She knew Patrick would feel even more guilty about Jake Rawnick than he already did when she told him. She picked up a sponge and ran it over the blue tile counter, rubbing at a nonexistent stain.

"There's been an unexpected complication," she said, squeezing the sponge dry and leaving it by the faucet. "Two guys who were on the run today work for the BLM. I don't think it's anything to—"

"What?" Patrick interrupted.

"I don't think it's anything to worry about.

They weren't sent to check on us," she assured him. "They were only there to raft."

"Are you sure?" he asked suspiciously. "Seems like quite a coincidence."

"Yes, it does." She nodded her agreement. "One of them followed me to the clearing, but I'd already finished the cleanup and was on the way back when he found me."

Patrick ran a hand over his chin. "That's just what we need. Who is this guy, anyway?"

"His name's Mark Wilde."

Patrick took a deep breath. "If the BLM gets wind of just how much damage Rawnick caused, we're up the Auburn with no paddle."

Maggie rolled her eyes. "You think I don't know that?"

"If it were only two or three complaints, we might slide by, but if they find out about the other problems—"

"I just wish *we* knew the full extent," she interrupted. "Or that Carl could tell us. I still don't understand why he didn't see something or have some inkling of what was going on. Wasn't he working with Rawnick?"

Patrick grimaced. "Carl's not as quick as he once was, Maggie, and Rawnick's a pro at deceit. He had me believing him too."

A muscle flicked angrily at her jaw and her brows drew down. "I saw that referral letter and it looked like the real thing to me," she said tersely. "Rawnick had it all figured out. He stole the letterhead, wrote and signed it himself, and got the job with us before the reference could be traced. He wanted a quick job and some quick money, and he got it. We just happened to be his target."

Taking a resigned breath, she went on. "And we can't blame Carl. He missed some obvious signs of trouble, but he has a heart of gold. He just isn't suspicious, and that's his only failing." She shrugged and gave Patrick a determined look.

"And now we'll get on with making things right," she assured him. "I picked up a lot of trash and dozens of dead seedlings today and filled in the gouges where Rawnick must have kicked them out of the ground. Some were three inches deep," she said sharply. Fear and anger knotted inside her—fear of losing their father's cherished permit and their business, and anger at the disaster Rawnick had created before disappearing without a trace.

"Patrick," Kerry called cheerily from the living room. "You must come and read this passage in my baby book."

"Gotta put on a smile for Kerry," he said. "She'd worry if she knew, and her time is too close."

Maggie stared wordlessly at Patrick and

watched him go to his wife. She realized just how much of this problem rested on her shoulders. Patrick's burden was heavy enough.

Mark knocked on the door of the director's office at ten o'clock on Monday morning and cracked it open. "You wanted to see me?" he asked the man sitting behind the desk, hunched over a stack of papers.

"Mark. Come in. Come in." Tom Bingham waved his hand in the air, then thumbed through the papers. "Ah, here it is." He pulled some paperclipped pages from the stack. Glancing up at Mark, he aimed his eyes over the top of his half-size reading glasses and sucked in his lower lip.

"New matter." Bingham punched his finger into the papers. "Important," he added tersely. "Requires one man working alone. How's your time?"

"I'm open."

"Good." Bingham took off his glasses and set them on the desk. "We've received complaints, several complaints, about an outfitter. The first notice for compliance went out ten days ago. I want a status report."

"What are the infractions?"

Bingham picked up his glasses, anchored them on his nose, and read from a document. "No safety instructions, flotation devices in disrepair.'' He turned to another page. "Trash and garbage left behind, cans and food tossed in the river.''

Mark frowned and leaned forward in his chair. "Who's pulling stunts like that?''

Bingham put up one hand. "There's more. Here's one from a man who went overboard and swam some rapids. Says he wasn't prepared. Didn't know what to do. Ended up with scrapes and abrasions and there was no first-aid kit in the raft.''

"What?'' Mark's mouth turned down even farther and lines appeared on his forehead. "Was the guy all right?''

"Apparently.'' Bingham flipped to another page. "More littering complaints, objectionable language, and improper behavior.'' He put down the papers and removed his glasses.

Mark scowled. "That outfitter's looking at stiff fines, maybe a suspension.''

Bingham pursed his lips. "That's not all. We have one letter that suggests—very strongly, I might add—that one of the guides carried a pistol.''

Mark's face paled. "An outfitter carrying a gun?''

Bingham sat back in his chair. "That's right.'' He stabbed his finger at the letter on his desk. "There's an implication that if we do some investigating, we just might find some dead animals. Apparently the guy went target practicing while the rafters took a break.''

''Any witnesses?''

Bingham shook his head. ''Afraid not. It was a half-day trip, one raft. The only testimony we've got is that shots were heard, and they were close by.''

Mark's scowl deepened. ''If that's true, the outfitter's permit is history. Do they know what they're up against?''

''They've been told it's serious, but not about the allegation of a firearm.'' Bingham paused and gestured in the air. ''I'll need corroboration to make it stick. This outfitter will be the first to come under the new regulations that went into effect last week, and I'm not inclined to be lenient.''

He pointed to the sheaf of papers. ''But there's something that doesn't quite add up. The outfitter has been in business a very long time and has a good reputation.'' He put the papers in a manila file folder, reached over the desk, and held it out to Mark. ''I want a thorough report by Monday.''

Mark stood up and took the papers.

''If you need help, Henderson is available.''

''Good. I'll be in touch if I need him.'' Mark turned and left, closing the office door behind him. He wouldn't have much time for the coalition this week. The investigation would be his top priority. He hadn't seen a complaint like this in a long time, and if they were true, he intended to make short shrift of the outfitter.

Opening the folder, he picked up the first letter. It was typewritten, two pages long. He skimmed the first paragraph and stopped and frowned. *It can't be. This is the last name I expected.* Whirling around, Mark walked back to the door he'd just closed, rapped on it, and entered when Bingham barked his admittance.

"Tom, there has to be some mistake. I was just on a run with Rapid Shooters and they knew what they were doing."

Bingham raised his eyebrows and peered over his glasses. "Was it a day run?"

"Yes, and I saw nothing to verify these charges."

"The incidents have been corroborated," Bingham reminded him. "Except the issue of the firearm."

"I tell you, one of the owners was on the run and she—"

Bingham narrowed his eyes to slits, scowled, and cut him off. "If you have a problem with this assignment, I can get Henderson—"

"The job's mine," Mark interrupted sharply.

Bingham leaned back in his chair, pressed his fingers together, and studied Mark over his glasses. "All right," he conceded. "I'll expect to hear from you first thing on Monday morning."

"Yes, sir," Mark answered before shutting the door behind him. He couldn't let Frank Henderson investigate Rapid Shooters. Henderson shut down everybody. Mark didn't know what was going on, but Maggie deserved a chance to explain. If he didn't get to the bottom of this, Rapid Shooters would be nothing more than a footnote in the bureau records. Their permit would be revoked and they'd be out of business.

Chapter Four

Maggie pulled into the parking lot of the nondescript office building at seven-fifteen on Tuesday night. She checked the address she'd written on the back of a tattered envelope. 220 Stockton Street. This had to be it.

She glanced up at the sun making its lazy descent to the horizon, then at the long shadows slanting across the dusty asphalt parking lot. *Late again*, she scolded herself. The meeting had already started. She found an empty space, pulled the car between faded white lines, and cut the motor. A shiny black Ranger was parked a few spaces away.

As she crossed in front of a large plate-glass window made hazy by the fading light, Maggie glimpsed thirty or forty people sitting in gray folding chairs, their attention fixed on a podium at the front of the room. Edging the door open, she found an empty chair in the fifth row. Her gaze was immediately drawn to the ruggedly handsome speaker standing at the front of the room.

He was writing something on the blackboard, his wide arm movements stretching his pale blue shirt across his back and emphasizing the broad muscles that tapered to a slim waist. His snug faded jeans were so worn, they hugged his hips like a second skin. She thought he looked more like a cowboy in a western movie than a government employee.

Mark turned around, pointing at the board with one hand and gesturing with the other. He was talking about the dam, ticking off numbers so fast that she didn't quite catch their significance, but it sounded like a string of statistics.

Cocking her head to one side, Maggie listened intently. After honing in on what he was saying, she thought that Mark certainly knew what he was talking about. His words had a ring of authority. She watched him scan the audience, his eyes widening when he saw her. She lowered her lashes, then met his chestnut-brown eyes head-on.

A smile playing at the corners of his mouth, he hesitated a moment, then quickly picked up his speech where he'd left off. "There are more than a hundred species of wildlife in the area where the dam will be built. Butterflies and bluejays." He waved one arm. "Owls, eagles, deer, elk . . .

a dozen species of fish. None are on the endangered species list. If they were, we'd have legal reasons for stopping construction of the dam.''

Mark walked a few steps to the left, then went back to the podium. Stretching his arms out straight in front of him, he anchored his palms against the edge of the lectern, standing with his legs angled wide. ''These animals nest and raise their young in the valleys and canyons. The cycle goes on as it has for centuries.'' He looked out at the audience again, his expression earnest.

''The Auburn is part of that cycle. It teems with life.'' He slid his arms across the podium and leaned on it. ''And people too. Settlers came in the 1700s, prospectors in the mid 1800s, middle America in the 1900s. Edgecreek, Sycamore Springs, and Parkerville were part of the Gold Rush, the days of the pioneer. That history should be protected.'' He paused, hooking a boot on a rung of the wooden stand and studying the audience.

Maggie's eyes locked on his. Everything about Mark radiated a deep intensity. He was determined and committed. She knew it, and so did the audience. She glanced around. Everyone watched him, heads craned forward with a sense of expectation. He literally had them on the edge of their chairs. Her pulse quickened and she knew

at that moment she would have followed him anywhere.

"The economies of the towns will change."
Mark paused to stare intently at the audience.
"But not for the better. The Auburn will be tamed.
Rafting and kayaking will be severely curtailed,
and wilderness camping will become a maze of
organized campgrounds." He held both hands
palm up then folded his arms across his chest and
lowered his voice.

"An enormous lake will be created behind the
dam. There'll be business and tourism, but instead
of rafting, kayaking, and fishing, we'll have RVs,
speedboats, and college kids with sports cars and
a case of beer in the cooler." He paced a few feet
in both directions, then faced forward and
stopped. "There will be business, but at what
cost?"

Maggie felt icy shafts of fear pierce her con-
sciousness. This was her home, her memories,
and—a blinding flash hit her—it was her future.
She was staying. She would fight to keep Sycamore Springs the way she remembered it, the way
it should remain.

Later that evening, Mark locked the door to the
building behind them. Everyone else had left.
"How about that cup of coffee?"

Maggie checked her watch. "It's after nine. I guess I have time."

"Terrific." He bent his head toward her, breathing in the sweet scent of her hair. She smelled like a meadow with the wildflowers just opening. As they walked across the darkened parking lot, Mark stifled an urge to drape an arm across her shoulders. Breathing a resigned sigh, he realized he was fighting a losing battle—he wanted nothing more on earth than to touch her. Slowly reaching out one hand, he gently cupped her shoulder, pulling her slightly closer.

Maggie glanced up, blinked, then eased away slightly.

Mark sighed. There was no getting around it. Maggie was an old-fashioned girl, whether he liked it or not. "There's a late-night diner over by the freeway," he said. "Best coffee and peach cobbler in town."

"Sounds good." She hesitated a moment when they reached her car. "Why don't I follow you?"

"Why don't you ride with me?"

She arched one brow. "So you won't have to drive me back if I decide to make a fast getaway."

Mark just shook his head. No point in making an issue out of her decision. "Whatever you say."

Maggie slid into the car, watching Mark saunter over to the Ranger, twirling his keys in the air. She heard the faint sound of a whistle echo through the still night and realized it came from Mark. She tilted one ear, listened, then smiled when she recognized another off-key Elvis tune, "Blue Suede Shoes."

A few minutes later she eased her car to a stop behind Mark's Ranger. The little diner was packed and she counted a dozen people sitting in the lounge area.

Mark opened his door and walked back to her car. "I'll see how long the wait is."

She nodded.

He was back in two minutes, hunkering down to eye level to talk. "Looks like at least thirty minutes. A couple of theaters just let out."

"Is there another coffee shop close by? It's getting late."

He thought for a minute. "No, not really, but I don't live far. I'm fresh out of pie, but I make great coffee."

Maggie hesitated, then realized a cup of coffee would help with the long drive home. "Sounds good," she decided.

"Make yourself comfortable," Mark said less than ten minutes later, closing the door behind them and switching on a tall brass table lamp. The small living room had a flagstone fireplace with a gold-framed painting of a forest scene hanging over it. A worn brown-tweed couch was angled in front of the hearth and a broad wing-back chair stood in one corner. Cream-colored shelves crammed tight with hundreds of books lined one wall and a CD player and speakers flanked the other.

"I'll start the coffee." He walked through a doorway that led to the kitchen, flicking on the light.

Maggie followed, leaning against the door when he opened the freezer.

"What would you like? French roast, Viennese, or Colombian?" he asked.

"You keep coffee in the freezer?"

"Yeah. That way I can find it."

Edging behind him, Maggie glanced in and shook her head. One frozen package of bagels and three TV dinners—all pot pies. "Viennese sounds nice," she said, hiding a smile.

Watching him pour the beans in the grinder, she stood on tiptoe to reach the filters perched precariously on top of the refrigerator. Handing him one, she recognized the feel of tough calluses on his hands when they touched. The sensation left her with an impression of strength and power, a feeling that was all male.

Mark took the filter, measured the grounds, slid the filter into the coffee maker, filled the reservoir with water, and turned it on. "This will only take a few minutes," he said.

Maggie wondered if he liked being a bachelor or just had a knack for making coffee. She opened her mouth to ask, decided against it, and turned and walked into the living room. Running her hand along the spines of the books lining the shelves, she picked one and flipped through the pages. Replacing it, she scanned the array of biographies, mysteries, and books on oceanography and ecology. She looked up and found him watching her.

"You must like reading too," she said.

"Always have." He leaned against the door frame and folded his arms across his chest.

"The Grand Canyon?" she asked, holding up a book.

"Gary and I did a five-day float down the Colorado last year."

He moved closer until he stood just inches away, so close that she caught a hint of his aftershave. It was a musky, bracing scent that reminded her of the forest after a light rain. "I've always wanted to raft the canyon."

"You should. There's nothing faster."

A grin lit her face. "I'd like that."

He grinned back. "I thought you might." They moved back to the kitchen. Mark poured two mugs of coffee, held one out, and steered her to the sofa. Dropping down beside her, close but not too close, he stretched his legs out and rested one foot on the edge of the coffee table.

"I saw you talking to Kay Rogers after the meeting," he said, taking a slug of coffee. "Did she convince you to volunteer for a committee?"

"She didn't have to do much convincing. I wanted to sign up for everything, but that'll have to wait until after Baby Macguire arrives. Right now, I'm a little short on time."

"There's a lot you can do from Sycamore Springs."

"Like what?"

"We need publicity. You could put posters and pamphlets in Outdoor Odyssey. A lot of people come through your store."

She shrugged, picked up the mug and took a sip. "That's easy."

"We could use help stuffing envelopes for mailings. We're always asking for contributions."

"That's easy too," she said, then caught herself before offering to do more. Until the mess with the BLM was straightened out, she didn't have any extra time, no matter how important the project was.

Mark smiled. "Good. I'll bring out everything you need to get started."

"To Sycamore Springs?" The question *why* leaped out at her, bringing back fears of an investigation. What business could Mark have in town on a weekday unless it had to do with his job?

He set his mug on the coffee table. "I'll be out your way Thursday. I'm taking off a long weekend to relax. Why don't we get together?"

She eyed him warily. "I've got a half-day run."

"How about dinner? We could go over the mailing lists and pamphlets afterward."

She paused. It might be a good idea if he and Patrick met. It would ease the tension a bit about the BLM. Maybe they'd get some answers. "Would you like to come to my house for dinner on Thursday?"

Mark licked his lips and breathed a contented sigh. "You don't have to ask twice," he said. "I'm a regular at every restaurant in town, and I *never* get my fill of home cooking."

"Good. It'll give me an excuse to make Kerry let me cook for a change."

"You need an excuse to invite me?" he teased.

"No." She laughed. "But I need an excuse to get Kerry out of the kitchen. She loves to cook."

"I bet you're a great cook too," he said confidently.

"Actually. . . . " She raised her brows. "I'm not."

He groaned. "What have I gotten myself into!"

"There's a reason," she insisted.

He put his hands up, palms flat. "Hey, not everybody likes to cook."

"No, it's not that." She shook her head. "I enjoy cooking, but I'm out of practice. I've been in the Philippines for the past two years."

"That's a long way from home. Why the trip?"

"I joined the Peace Corps after college, decided to see the world." She laughed, remembering the small village she'd called home. Not exactly the world. "I taught English to village children."

"You're a teacher?"

"No, but that's where I was needed. I managed to get involved in other things too. I helped modernize some of their agricultural methods and establish a system of wells for the village."

"Now, that sounds like something you'd enjoy."

"Enjoy, my eye! I did it out of desperation. It was a four-mile walk to the river to bathe, wash my clothes, *and* carry back my drinking water. I decided there had to be a better way." She rolled her eyes, then drained her coffee.

"It sounds primitive."

She nodded. "The village was very remote and only the children spoke English, but the work kept me so busy I never got lonely. I had my own hut and a small cooking stove, but the diet was mainly rice, fruit, and vegetables." She turned toward him and sighed. "Which is why I haven't cooked in ages."

He shook his head in mock panic. "And you're going to practice on me?"

"Yes," she insisted, putting her mug on the table next to his, then shaking her finger at him. "And you have to promise not to complain."

"I promise," he said, nodding.

She sighed and checked her watch. "I should be going. I have an early rafting trip tomorrow."

He put a hand to her chin and turned her face so she was looking into his eyes as he leaned closer. "How early?"

"Very early," she answered as she watched Mark's face come closer. Her eyes slid closed as his mouth covered hers like a soft velvet cloak, then his arms folded around her back. She couldn't remember being kissed that way before—the sensations were both tender and strong at the same time.

She told herself a kiss couldn't be wrong, remembering that two years was a very long time and she *was* human. Even as she listened to the voice deep inside her that warned her away from Mark, she was irresistibly drawn closer. Then the past came back, pushing between them like a wall of steel. Maggie stiffened her shoulders, then twisted away.

"What's wrong?" he asked, clearly puzzled.

She didn't know what to make of the situation, or of what she was doing. She'd sworn she wouldn't get involved with a man outside of marriage, yet here she was in Mark's living room, letting him kiss her and kissing him back.

"Nothing's wrong," she insisted. "But it's time for me to go." She forced herself to stand.

Mark reached for her hand and didn't let go. "Will I see you next week?"

She nodded slowly, pulled her hand free, and stepped toward the door. "Good night," she murmured stiffly, reached for the doorknob, and walked into the night.

Mark stood on the porch, watching the taillights on Maggie's car fade to glimmers in the dark night. When he closed the door behind him, the place seemed empty. With a heavy sigh, he decided to see Bingham first thing in the morning and resign from the case. There was no way he could investigate Maggie's company. Not after tonight.

Mark whipped the rubber band off the morning newspaper and flicked open the front section. He repeatedly drew his thumb up and down the crease that separated the pages until it was smoothed flat against the kitchen table. It had been the longest two nights of his life. The hours between Tuesday and Thursday had seemed to stretch into the distance like a never-ending, desolate savanna.

Bingham had agreed to take Mark off the case and reassign it to Frank Henderson. Since Mark had already signed himself out for two vacation days, he had decided to head to Sycamore Springs to get a handle on the situation before Henderson showed up.

Picking up the phone, he'd dialed the Forty-Niner Motel in Sycamore Springs and changed his reservation to include Sunday night. If he finished on Saturday, he hoped to spend Sunday with Maggie. He'd called her last night, but he only reached Patrick, who hadn't given a hint of where she was or when she'd be home. Mark had left a message, then stayed up reading until midnight, but she didn't return his call. Unable to sleep, he'd finally given up and started driving north at six-thirty.

He'd spent the morning tramping through the forest that edged the banks of the Auburn, up in the high stretches where the river ran strong and fast. The day was warm, the sky an electric blue, and the clean smell of pine and spruce filled his lungs at every step. He would give anything to live up here away from the city. The city was choking him.

By early afternoon, he'd identified three of Rapid Shooters's put-in sites and examined every inch of underbrush until he found what he was looking for—evidence of the name of the outfitter responsible for the rubbish he'd meticulously sifted through. He'd found typewritten release forms at two sites. They were tattered and ground into the dirt, but he could still make out the bright yellow Rapid Shooter logo and most of the names and dates.

He had recognized two names—Sutherland and Thompson. They'd both sent letters to the BLM complaining about Jake Rawnick. Mark had left the evidence at the sites—let Henderson do his own legwork. It was Maggie who needed help, and the case for Rapid Shooters didn't look very good.

The third site appeared to have been scrupulously cleaned. The underbrush was swept free of leaves and pine needles, and the scrub grass was so neat it looked as if it had been combed.

Twenty or so seedlings had been newly planted and tapped into the earth. There wasn't a scrap of paper, empty can, or solitary piece of litter anywhere.

Maggie must have gotten there first, he decided, wishing he could let her fix things and leave it at that. But he knew questions had to be answered, rules had to be obeyed, penalties had to be paid. Henderson would see to that. The man was like a newspaper. Black and white—no gray. He didn't believe in excuses, extenuating circumstances, or margins for error. The fact that Rawn-ick had been employed by Rapid Shooters would be reason enough for Henderson to recommend they be closed down.

It was after six that evening when Mark crossed the wide wooden porch of the two-story Victorian and knocked on the front door. When Maggie answered, her eyes opened wide with surprise. "You came," she said, her voice breaking.

"When you didn't return my call, I didn't know what—"

"I-I was busy."

His eyes registered her confusion, which made no sense to him. In fact, nothing was making sense. The thought rang through his head that all he'd thought about for the last two days was Mag-gie, and she hadn't done the same. He felt as if she'd punched him, hard.

"Am I invited to dinner or not?" he asked, a dark scowl hiding his bruised feelings.

"Of course you are," she answered in a rush, as if he shouldn't have doubted the invitation. "I've been planning on it all day. I just didn't have time to call."

She bit down on her lower lip, realizing she couldn't tell him the real reason—that she'd been afraid he wouldn't show up; that she would react to Mark the same way she had with Todd. She'd been attracted to her college sweetheart in that mind-numbing way too, and she'd let romance, rather than reason, rule her heart. She might as well get it over with and tell Mark the whole story before she fell into the same trap. She opened the screen door and stepped outside.

The warm stillness enveloped her. She walked over to the porch railing, leaned against it, then took a deep breath. She squared her shoulders and swallowed. "Mark, there's no point in seeing each other again. It can't go anywhere."

For a minute, he didn't answer. Then she heard his voice, cold and harsh. "What is it that can't go anywhere, Maggie?"

"You and me," she said in a quiet, resigned voice.

He moved behind her, turning her around until she faced him. "What are you talking about? There's already something going on between us. Or at least there is for me."

She wanted to deny the truth of what he said, but she couldn't. It had been easy to push aside thoughts of romance when she was in the Philippines, but she seemed to fall in love as easily as another woman might accept a dinner date— and always with the wrong man. She turned around, leaning against the railing as if for support, then answered, "You're wrong, Mark. There's nothing between us."

"Nothing?" He ran a hand through his hair,

then said gruffly, "All the signs are there, Maggie. You just won't admit it. And if I'm wrong about that, then you're sending mixed signals. And that's a little girl's game."

She looked up then. Her eyes were calm again, calm and direct. Whatever fears that swirled inside her were under control. There was nothing she was afraid of. Not the eerie night sounds of the jungle, not treacherous, boiling white water, not even being alone. But she was terrified of how Mark made her feel, and she was terrified of falling in love. That was what Todd had done to her. She stared into the night an instant longer, then took a deep breath.

"I don't play little girl games, Mark," she whispered. "But I'm not sure I want to find out where we're headed."

He stiffened as though she had struck him. "Why not, Maggie? What are you afraid of?"

"Oh, my!" a lilting female voice interrupted.

Kerry stood just inside the doorway, a grin plastered across her face. "You must be Mark, and you're joining us for supper."

He looked down at Maggie, who blushed scarlet, then turned back around and smiled politely. "And you must be Kerry."

"Well, now, who else would I be?" Kerry chuckled and patted her stomach. "Come along and meet Patrick." She held the screen door open.

Maggie's shoulders drooped. She'd wanted to tell Mark, get it all out in the open, but instead she'd started an argument. She gave him a solemn look. "We'll talk later."

"That we will," he agreed, taking her hand.

As they made their way through the house, Kerry kept up her usual steady stream of chatter. "You two go on ahead," Maggie said when they reached the kitchen. "I've got some cooking to do."

Kerry took Mark's arm. "Come outside and chat with Patrick and me."

Maggie folded her arms across her chest and shook her head. She wished Kerry hadn't interrupted their conversation; she wished it hadn't ended on a bad note. Worse yet, Maggie knew Kerry would ask Mark a string of questions aimed at deciding if he was husband material. Her sister-in-law believed Prince Charming was waiting right around the corner, but Maggie had her doubts. Todd had shown her that the glass slipper came in a size six, and she knew her foot was definitely a size eight.

She let out a big sigh and followed them into the backyard. Maybe she could distract Kerry. When she stepped outside, she knew it was too late. They were headed for the lower part of the yard toward Kerry's twenty-row vegetable garden. If there was one subject Maggie didn't intrude on, it was the virtues of organic farming. Last year Kerry had won prizes at the county fair for strawberries, three kinds of lettuce, and two varieties of squash. If she heard one more discourse on the benefits of a compost heap, she'd die. Mark would have to fend for himself.

An hour later, Maggie blew her bangs off her forehead with a hard blast of air while stirring sauce with one hand and testing pasta with the other. She was glad she'd settled on a simple meal of salad, spaghetti, and garlic bread. She glanced out the kitchen window at Mark, Patrick, and Kerry. They were talking and laughing like chums who'd shared a day riding the rapids. When Mark had come in and offered to help, she'd shooed him out of the kitchen. Now she regretted it. They were obviously having fun, and she felt left out.

Wrinkling her nose, she made a mad dash for the stove and threw open the oven door. Darn! Sliding out the rack, she saw that only the top of the loaf had burned. A quick slice would take care of it.

She leaned out of the window. "Dinner's ready. Everybody inside. Patrick, would you open a bottle of Chianti?"

The crustless loaf went in the bread basket, the salad was tossed, and the spaghetti sauce ladled. Maggie glanced at the clock on the wall as she joined the others in the dining room and slipped into her chair. Eight o'clock. *Not bad*, she complimented herself. *Not bad at all.*

"Smells wonderful," Mark commented as he helped himself to pasta. "I'm starved."

Maggie was halfway through her salad when Mark made a strangled sound once, then again. He put a hand to his mouth and made the sound again, then ran a finger around the edge of his collar. His face turned beet red.

"Is anything wrong?" she asked.

"No." He coughed, then took a big gulp of water.

Kerry put some pasta in her mouth, then reached for her water glass.

"What is it?" Maggie glanced around the table again.

"Uhm, uhm." Patrick cleared his throat. "A little too much garlic, Sis."

"Too much garlic? The recipe said two cloves. That's what I put in."

"Maggie, dear," Kerry said between gulps of water, "this sauce has more than two cloves in it."

"I put in two cloves," she insisted. "That's all I found in the fridge."

Kerry's fork clattered to her plate. "But those were *heads* of garlic, not *cloves*." She giggled, pressing her hands to her cheeks.

Maggie felt her face redden. "But I thought. . . . "

"No harm done," Kerry said, pushing her chair out from the table. "I have some fresh basil. Won't take two minutes in the food processor and we'll have a nice pesto sauce for the spaghetti."

Patrick turned to Mark, still all smiles, and he shook his head. "Maggie never did learn to cook. After my mother died, she gave it a whirl, but. . . . " He shrugged and turned his palms up. "I usually got stuck with the chore. Either that or starve."

Maggie glowered at Patrick. "And what was wrong with you doing the cooking?"

Patrick's smile got bigger and he shook his head. "Not a thing, sis. Not a thing."

Mark reached over and cupped his hand over Maggie's. "The pasta is cooked perfectly . . . just the way I like it. And the salad is great."

Maggie glanced sideways at him, one side of her mouth turning up a notch.

He squeezed her hand. "Maggie, I *love* garlic!"

She finally gave up and grinned. She knew she couldn't defend her cooking. Pinches, bunches, cloves, heads . . . how could anyone remember which was which?

Patrick pushed himself away from the table,

went over to Maggie, and ruffled her hair. "I'm going to help Kerry. Keep your beau company."

Maggie glanced at Mark and felt her pulse quicken, then steady. No way. Mark wasn't her beau. Not after tonight.

"I'm sure if I just sit for a minute, I'll be fine. Just fine," Kerry insisted an hour later, still shaking from a contraction that had nearly knocked her off her feet.

Patrick had one arm around her waist, leading her to the sofa. "Do you think it's time, sweetheart?"

Kerry shook her head. "No. I saw Dr. Girard yesterday and he said another week. Maybe longer." She fell onto the couch and laid her head back, both hands falling to her stomach. "I'm just tired."

Maggie came in with a cold cloth and pressed it to Kerry's forehead. Her skin was damp with sweat. She reached around and took Kerry's hand, feeling her pulse. "Should we call the doctor?"

"I tell you, I'm fine," Kerry insisted.

Maggie looked at Patrick and swallowed hard. His face was ashen. She thought she recognized the look of fear in his eyes.

Just then Kerry doubled over with another contraction.

Patrick reached for his wife.

Maggie grabbed the telephone.

Mark bolted for the door.

Chapter Five

"**I**'ll pull the Ranger into the driveway," Mark yelled over his shoulder.

Twenty minutes later Patrick stopped pacing the hospital floor and asked for the third time, "Why is it taking so long? Why can't I be with her?"

"I'm sure the doctor will be out in a minute," Maggie repeated for the third time. "He just wanted you to leave for the exam." Maggie looked up and met Mark's eyes. He moved closer and draped one arm around her waist.

Dr. Girard opened the door and motioned Patrick into the examining room.

"Coffee?" she suggested.

"No caffeine for me." Mark yawned. "I'm hoping to get some sleep tonight."

"You aren't sleeping?"

"It's the motel. Spent too many nights in them

when I was a kid. Never managed to sleep very well.''

''Your parents traveled a lot?''

He shrugged. ''I guess you could say that. I spent the school year with my father and summers with Mom. Dad was a salesman and peddled any number of things on the dusty, small-town circuit. We spent a lot of time driving.''

''Your parents were divorced?''

''When I was eight.''

She looked up at him, seeing the pained look in his eyes. Her childhood memories were so different from the ones Mark described. His sounded hard and strained. Hers were all light and wonderful. ''I can't imagine living in two places,'' she said. ''Or not having my mother and father together.''

Running a hand over his chin, Mark blinked several times, then said, ''It was tough. I loved them both and I always felt torn between them. I never really felt like I had a home to call mine. I was always moving between two houses, two sets of friends, two sets of rules.''

Just as Maggie was trying to think of something to say to Mark, Dr. Girard came out of Kerry's room and approached them. ''It's a false alarm, but unless I miss my guess, we'll have a baby any day now. Keep an eye on your sister-in-law," he cautioned. "She tends to overdo."

Maggie nodded. "She's got a mind of her own, you know."

"Yes." Dr. Girard nodded. "I do. I've been trying to get her off her feet for a week now, but I haven't had much success. Just do your best. I'll drop by the house and see her tomorrow morning," he added before leaving.

Maggie relaxed her shoulders and felt Mark's arm tighten around her.

"Imagine—a town where doctors still make house calls," he noted in amazement.

She smiled. "Dr. Girard's the best. He knows all about babies."

Mark pushed back a wisp of hair from her eyes, then said, "This is just the beginning for your brother and Kerry."

Maggie looked puzzled. "The beginning? The doctor said Kerry wasn't in labor."

"No." He shook his head. "I mean the whole parenthood business. That'll take up every minute they have. I can't imagine what it would be like to have children underfoot all the time."

Maggie smiled. "You don't understand. Once a couple has a baby, that's all they want time for."

"Are you so sure about that?"

She gave him a quizzical look. "Of course I'm sure."

Mark pursed his lips. "Maybe," he said, wondering how parents could divorce if that were really true. Mark put his arms out and eased Maggie into his embrace. In that moment he felt closer to her than he thought possible. The ache in his heart told him he cared more than he'd planned to, and there'd be no turning back if he didn't start down the road pretty quickly. But he knew he wasn't ready for commitment or a family. He didn't know if he ever would be.

By the time he drove Maggie, Kerry, and Patrick home and made his way back to the motel on the edge of town, it was past midnight. Sleep was impossible, so he worked on a few angles to get Maggie out of her predicament with the BLM. He only wished there was something he could do to thwart Henderson's usually thorough job. Nothing against regulations. Nothing unethical. Just a slightly gray smoke screen.

He woke with a start sometime during the night, hunched over the desk, pencil still clutched in his hand. He still hated motel rooms. He had spent too many nights in them and had never managed a decent night's sleep. He trudged over to the bed, pulled his boots off, stretched out on the too-soft mattress, and punched the mini pillow.

Before dozing off, he decided the only way he'd

get some sleep was to find a quiet spot on the river tomorrow and camp out. He always kept a bedroll, a two-man tent, and camping and fishing gear in the Ranger, and he knew the sound of the river would lull him to sleep like a baby.

Putting aside the sheaf of papers he'd been working on, Mark stood up and stretched. After hiking in that morning, he'd discovered a spot a dozen yards from the riverbank and set up camp under the branches of a towering California redwood. Now the sun was high overhead.

The Auburn was quiet here as it wound lazily through the timberland. He felt as if he could stay forever. Peace and quiet. It was all he'd needed to feel like himself again. Walking down to the river, he passed tiny white flowers growing wild amidst patches of soft grass. When he reached the river's edge, he bent down, cupped water in his hands, then sluiced it over his head.

A good sight better than a motel, he told himself for the tenth time since staking his tent. Gazing into the sparkling clear water, he detected movement under the surface. The thought of trout cooking over a wood fire sent his taste buds into high gear, and he decided to fetch his rod and reel. Standing up, he jerked back and stopped himself just before swinging his fist around.

The sound of a woman's shriek pierced the air.

"Maggie!" He righted himself. "My God. Don't walk up on a man like that, with no warning."

She put one hand to her heart and took a deep breath. "I didn't see you. You scared me half out of my wits."

He reached out both hands and held her until she steadied. "Are you okay?"

"I think so." She felt her heart slow from the breakneck speed it had hit when she'd seen him, then bolt again. "What are you doing out here?" she asked. "The nearest road is more than a mile away."

"Camping," he said. "I finally gave up on the motel and drove out this morning." His expression turned serious. "How's Kerry?"

"Fine. She was still sleeping when I left this morning."

"Were you hiking?" he asked.

She bit down on her lower lip and crossed her fingers behind her back. "Yes, along a rough trail just over there. I got hot and came down for a drink." She hadn't been hiking. She'd been upriver to a spot Rawnick had trashed. And she was lying—again. Apparently she was getting quite good at it, and she didn't like that either.

"How about some lemonade?" Mark asked, his voice gruff and unsure. Maggie wore a simple white cotton shirt and faded thigh-high cutoffs.

She looked so pretty, he wanted to kiss her, and since he couldn't, he had to get his mind on something else—like lemonade. He took her hand and started toward camp, pointing to the area he had chosen for himself. "Here we are."

Almost hidden from view by the sweep of lacy redwood branches, the tent was only partially visible. A folding table and camp stools were set up close by. Fresh firewood was stacked by the tent and a kerosene lantern and a dented coffeepot sat on one of the rocks that comprised the fire pit. He reached into a cooler, brought out a Thermos, and poured lemonade into plastic cups.

He pointed at her nose and grinned. "Looks like you got some sun. I think I can count more freckles than you had the other day."

She cocked one brow and pushed back her hair with both hands. "Probably. It's hot today."

Mark swallowed, watching her hands move in her hair. He had to get his mind off taking Maggie in his arms and kissing her. Talking about business would do just that, but he wondered how he was going to tell her. He'd tried to keep his job out of their relationship, but it simply wasn't possible. He knew he had to tell her.

"Maggie," he said gently. "Do you trust me?"

Her face clouded with old fears and uncertainties. "You haven't given me any reason not to," she said cautiously.

Mark closed his eyes for an instant, then paced a few feet in both directions, looked at her, then paced again. *Good. She trusts me. That's a good sign. Now if only she'll listen.* Finally he turned to her. "I didn't come up here just for a long weekend." He ran a hand over his neck. "You know I mentioned the BLM is shorthanded during the summer."

She nodded.

"I've been helping with some of the legwork on the routine investigations." He hooked his fingers in his back pockets and stared out at the river, then squared his shoulders and turned around. "The director assigned me to a new case last week. I wish I could've told you before, and I guess there's no easy way to do it now." He ran a hand over his chin. "Maggie, I know all about Jake Rawnick and the charges against Rapid Shooters—"

"What?" At first she felt shaken, then angry. "You mean, the notice we got making accusations, asking all those questions?"

"That's the one. They assigned me to investigate your company."

It hit her all at once, but she shook her head in swift denial. It couldn't be true. Surely he would have told her before now. She stood up. "And you said nothing?"

He reached out and grabbed her arm. "Maggie—"

She whirled around, trying to throw his arm off, but he held on. Her eyes were like pinpoints, flashing the hurt and anger that threatened to consume her. He was just another good-looking man with a honeyed tongue and clever hands. The world was full of them, and she was apparently destined to run a search-and-rescue mission to find every one.

Mark tightened his grip on her arm. "Maggie, I took myself off the case."

She took a quick, sharp breath. "Why?"

"Regulations. If I'd stayed on the case, I couldn't see you." He let go of her arm and looked away. "Not if I wanted to keep my job. I know what you've been doing. The replanting, carrying out trash—"

"How do you know about that?"

"I've been to your put-in sites and the places along the river where I thought Rawnick might have ported."

"You've been following me?"

He shook his head vehemently. "No. I've been trying to help. I've been one step behind you, and I've gone to a few places you haven't been."

Maggie jerked her head back, then spit out, "You'd think I'd learned a thing or two, but apparently not. There's just no trusting men. I'm getting out of here.''

He grabbed her hand. ''Just a minute—''

''No!'' She jerked her hand free. ''You wait a minute. I don't find the fact that you followed me—spied on me—very amusing.''

''Neither would I, if that's what I'd been doing, but I wasn't.'' He moved close and tried to take her hand, but she folded her arms across her chest.

''I told you, I'm trying to *help*. And what's this about not trusting men?''

She laughed, a cold, sinister sound. ''What's to trust? You're all alike.''

''Maggie, I'm sorry if someone hurt you or betrayed your trust, but it doesn't have anything to do with me. Give me a break.''

His bitter sarcasm hit her like a jolt. She tried to force her confused emotions into a semblance of order, but she found it impossible. She'd trusted again and discovered a web of deceit. And he'd blown it off like a whim. What more did she need to know? She gave him a sidelong glance. ''I don't want to talk about it.''

Mark glowered at her. ''I'm not ready to let you walk out without a fight. You're going to talk, whether you like it or not.''

''Excuse me?'' she spluttered. ''Why should I talk to you about anything?''

''A better question is why not?''

Her mouth dropped. Such a simple question. It hit her head-on, like a hurricane. She faced him. They might as well get it all out in the open. Let him prove his true colors, just like Todd.

"All right. I'll tell you. I fell in love when I was in college." Her voice sounded strained as a vivid recollection passed through her mind. The happiness, the disbelief, the anger. "We were engaged, we planned our life together. He said he loved me, wanted to get married. I believed him." She frowned. "I planned a summer wedding, a long white dress. . . . " The last words came out in a mumble, her eyes glistening. She swallowed hard, intent on keeping her voice from breaking. "A few days after he slipped a ring on my finger, I found him with another woman."

Mark took a step forward and put his arms around her, enveloping her with his body, taking the pain from her and absorbing it. "But that was years ago. And college guys are as hormonal as they come. Believe me. I remember."

"I bet you do," she said, her eyes cold and passionless. "He was handsome and charming, and I fell for him hook, line, and sinker. And he betrayed me." She leaned back and faced Mark. "And it's happened again. You lied to me, and now you expect me to trust you?"

"Maggie, don't you think you're jumping the gun a bit here?"

"No. No, I don't. You lied to me."

He ran a hand through his hair, dark strands falling on his forehead. "I had my reasons. My job. I explained all that. And you still don't understand?"

"No, I guess I don't."

He took a step back and stared at her. Her eyes were unforgiving. She hadn't listened to a word he'd said; she'd already made up her mind. "Fine," he said tersely. "If that's the way you want it." He turned around and walked toward the tent. He started loading the Ranger with his camping gear. When he'd calmed down a minute later and decided to apologize, she'd disappeared.

Mark knocked on Frank Henderson's door at ten o'clock on Monday morning. When he got no response, he edged open the door and looked in. Henderson was hunched over his desk, the phone receiver held tightly against one ear. He saw Mark in the doorway and waved him in.

A minute later he slammed the receiver down and stared at the telephone. "It's only Monday and already my week is screwed up." He glanced at Mark. "What's up?"

"Rapid Shooters." Mark settled into a chair. "I spent quite a lot of time on the Auburn last week checking their put-in sites and hiking thirteen or fourteen miles of their route."

Henderson leaned back in his chair. "What's your interest?"

"I'm going to level with you, Frank. One of the owners is a friend of mine. That's why I took myself off the case. But I think they've been railroaded."

Henderson tapped a folder on his desk. "It looks pretty cut-and-dried to me."

"What about Jake Rawnick?"

Henderson shrugged. "The bureau rules say if he's an employee, the owners are liable. Doesn't matter that he did the dirty work."

"Are you going to give the outfitter a chance to explain?"

Henderson leaned forward, a dark frown creasing his face. "Level with me, Mark. It isn't like you to ask for favors when a company's responsible for this kind of damage. You'd throw the book at them, same as me."

"I want this guy, Frank. I want him bad. He's responsible, not the outfitter. I want blame laid where it belongs."

"That's understandable, Mark, but—"

"Frank, you don't know the worst of it. At two places near the river I found some small animals and birds that had been shot."

Henderson's look turned dark. "Bingham told me about the firearm."

"He told you right. I counted a dozen bullet

holes in some carcasses.'' Leaning forward in his chair, Mark shook his head. ''The guy must have been target practicing. I thought the department might want some evidence, so I brought back a few. Buried the rest. All told, there were a couple dozen blue jays, a pair of ospreys, squirrels, and a doe. The only thing I can figure is that he must have carried a small-caliber handgun.''

Henderson's eyes widened. ''Do you think it's possible he carried it when he took people down the river? When he worked for the outfitter?''

''You bet I do, only we don't have a witness. We need someone to testify that they *saw* him.'' Mark reached into his back pocket, retrieved a small object, and held it out. ''Take a look.''

Henderson took the lighter and turned it over, read the inscription, then looked at Mark. ''Nice work. Very nice indeed.'' He held the lighter up and read, *''To Jake. Happy Birthday. 6-4-90.''* He turned it over again. ''Where did you find this?''

''Same place I found the dead ospreys.''

''Have you verified the birth date with the outfitter?''

Mark's jaw unclenched. ''Remember—I'm not on the case.''

Henderson looked up and met Mark's direct gaze. A subtle look of understanding passed between them. "I'll make the call. Part of my investigation. I'm going out tomorrow."

"Could you delay until next week? The outfitter's working on a project that may affect your investigation."

He gave Mark a hard look. "I'll drive out next Tuesday morning. That's all the time I can give you."

"Thanks, Frank."

"I don't want thanks, buddy. I want this case put to rest."

As Mark walked down the narrow hallway, he mentally checked off what needed to be done. His thoughts turned again to a decision he'd been gnawing on for the past week or so—whether this would be the last investigation he worked on, officially or otherwise. He'd never intended to spend his life enforcing government regulations, and he'd had enough.

That's not why he'd majored in environmental studies at Berkeley, and not why he'd decided to stay in California. The state was a watershed of new ideas and theories about the planet and how to protect it. He wanted to make a difference in at least a small corner of the world.

His thoughts drifted to the coalition. He felt a rush just thinking about the issues they were involved in and the new world order he saw emerging. One world, one people, committed to saving itself from destruction so another generation could safely inhabit the planet. It would be a dream to spend all his time with the coalition, but it wasn't feasible. At least, not right now. He still had to buy groceries and pay the rent.

"Hey, Mark," Gary greeted him from down the hallway.

"How's it going?" Mark asked as the two men shook hands.

Gary raised his brows. "Bingham's kept us hopping all week. Where've you been hiding?"

"Out around Sycamore Springs doing some fieldwork. Let's grab a cup of coffee, pal. I'd like to talk to you about something."

They made their way to the lunchroom, poured mugs of thick, bitter coffee, and went down another hallway to Mark's office. He closed the door behind them, sat in his worn leather chair, and took a slug.

"I need your help with something important, Gary."

"Is it coalition business?"

"Not yet, but I'm hoping to get them involved. In fact, you could help by making a few phone calls. I want this set up before the meeting tonight."

Gary grabbed a sheet of paper and a pencil, moistened the tip on his tongue, and poised it over the paper. "Who do you want me to call?"

* * *

"It's nice having you working at home this afternoon, Maggie," Kerry said, looking down at her knitting and counting the stitches on the tiny white sweater before turning the piece over.

Maggie stuffed another envelope with a brightly colored flyer, then added it to a box that held similar rows of envelopes, all stamped with the California Rivers Coalition return address. "I can do this here as easily as I can at the store. It goes fairly quickly once you get started."

"You're going to finish all that today?"

Maggie nodded, placing another envelope in the brown cardboard box. "I'm taking them to Sacramento tonight."

Maggie saw the look in Kerry's eyes and knew what she was thinking. She chewed on her lower lip. "Since it doesn't look like Baby Macguire is going to show up tonight, I thought I'd risk the drive to Sacramento. There's a coalition meeting."

Kerry rested her knitting on her abdomen. "You've taken a sudden interest in this coalition."

Maggie nodded, trying to keep her voice low. "It's an important project."

"Yes," Kerry agreed. "I just thought it might be the *man* you were interested in."

Maggie stuffed two pieces of paper into an envelope. She had to be careful. If Kerry knew that she cared for Mark, she wouldn't have a moment's peace until a wedding date was set. *What a laugh that is*, she thought wryly. *And I'm not in the mood for any girl talk. There's no point.*

But Kerry wasn't to be put off. "Maggie, what's going on between you and Mark?"

Maggie sighed. She'd have to tell her something. Kerry wasn't going to leave her alone until she did. "Mark and I have been seeing each other," she said slowly. "But it doesn't—"

Kerry jumped out of her chair, rushed over to Maggie, and threw her arms around her. "Oh, Maggie. I thought you looked even prettier than usual. Now I know why."

Maggie frowned. "Wait a minute, Kerry. It's not like that. Believe me, Mark and I aren't—"

Kerry took Maggie's hand and pulled her toward the antique mirror hanging in the hallway. "Just take a look!" She peered into the mirror with Maggie. "Don't you know love when you see it?"

Maggie frowned and sucked in her lips. She knew her sister-in-law was an impossible romantic, but this was too much. "I am *not* in love." She started to move away, but Kerry pulled her back. She glanced at her image in the mirror again. Her skin looked tanned, with the usual sprinkling of summer freckles marching across the bridge of her nose and under both eyes. She wore no makeup and no blusher, but her cheeks did seem to have a rosy tinge.

Her eyes met Kerry's in the mirror. "This is silly—another one of your fanciful ideas. There's nothing more different today than any other day, and I look just the same." She pointed toward her mouth. "See! My front tooth is *still* crooked."

Kerry let out a peal of laughter. "Silly, I'm not talking about your teeth. Mark's so tall and handsome. Smart too." She rolled her eyes. "Just think of the babies you'll have."

Maggie's mouth dropped. "Kerry!" She grabbed her backpack from the closet, set it on the table, and deposited several stacks of envelopes inside. "I'm going down to the store so I can get some work done!"

Her thoughts wandered as she quickly covered the four short blocks between home and town. The sun shone brightly overhead and the fragrant scent of roses filled the summer air. She decided to forget all about Kerry and her talk of love.

A smile lit her face when she approached the store and saw the tidy sign with white letters that read OUTDOOR ODYSSEY. Her father had redesigned it a few months before he died, drawing the Os with long, curly tails.

''Excuse me.''

Maggie turned at the words. A man she didn't know stood a few feet away, a thin grin softening his somewhat harsh features.

Chapter Six

Maggie gave him a friendly smile. He was probably a tourist in need of directions.

The man pointed toward the store. "Were you going in there—that outfit that takes people down the river?"

"Yes. I'm Maggie Macguire, one of the owners. Were you interested in booking a trip?"

His smile straightened, and his bushy eyebrows slanted down. "Uh, no. I wasn't." He sucked in his lips. "Just wondered if they were open. Some stores close up come lunchtime."

"No, we're open. Were you looking for backpacking equipment or fishing gear?" she asked, hoping he was a potential customer. They needed the business.

"Uh, yes. Yes, I was, but I got to meet my friend down by the fire station. We'll come on back up, now I know you're open." He gave her an odd look, then continued down the street.

Funny, he was headed away from the fire station. Probably confused. "Mister," she called out, raising one hand to wave at him. When he didn't answer, she decided he hadn't heard her. Someone would surely point him in the right direction.

Maggie started across the street, then looked back at the figure retreating in the distance. *An odd-looking man*, she thought, watching him walk along. His head angled out ahead of his body, almost like a bird staring at the ground, ready to peck at a fat, juicy worm.

A few minutes later, she opened the door to Outdoor Odyssey, glad to see Patrick busy with two customers. Business seemed to be picking up. She set her backpack behind the counter and went back outside and around the building to the shed. She was looking for a hammer.

When she opened the door, she frowned. What a mess. Neither she nor Patrick was the tidy sort, and he must have been in the shed looking for something. The trash bags she'd brought back from the river were open, and she distinctly remembered tying them closed with pieces of string. She'd been annoyed when she couldn't find scissors to cut the string, finally resorting to dull garden shears.

Rummaging around in a cabinet, she eventually found a hammer and some nails, then went back inside the store. Positioning four nails between her lips, she unrolled a coalition poster and pounded the nails into the wall. After arranging some pamphlets on the counter, she walked across the room to the catchall drawer and dropped the hammer inside.

"Any sales?" she asked Patrick.

"Not bad for a Monday. We've got daily runs booked into next month and I've scheduled a guide's course for July."

"Good. You know, I didn't realize how much I missed rafting until I came back." She paused for a heartbeat. "I always think of white water in connection with Dad." She looked at Patrick, her eyes bright. "I sure miss him."

He came over and put an arm around her shoulder. "Dad was so proud of you for joining the Peace Corps. He always talked about his little girl, off in the jungle, teaching children."

"Well, I'm back now." She squared her shoulders. "And I'll be glad when we get this mess with the BLM cleared up so we can focus on the business."

"Me too, sis. Carl's found a new guide to help out through the season. He came in this morning."

She leaned against the wall and shoved her hands in her back pockets. "Patrick, I've been wanting to talk to you about Carl."

"What about him?"

"He had trouble keeping up with me on the last run. I think it's time he quit white water."

Patrick gave her a resigned look. "I haven't wanted to think about it, but you're right."

She paced a few feet in one direction. "There's something else too. Carl should've seen what Rawnick was doing. He went on most of his runs."

"I know, Maggie, but it's not Carl's fault. I'm responsible for keeping things straight, and I didn't."

She closed her eyes. "There's no point in laying blame. We have to make sure we're covered now." She paused, then went on. "I'm sure Carl will understand. There's still a lot he can do, but we can't keep him in a position of authority."

Patrick glanced at her. "I'm not so sure how he's going to feel about it, but I agree we don't have any choice. I can keep him busy just helping out in the store. I've been so caught up with Kerry and, what with the baby coming—"

"And the house, Outdoor Odyssey, and the legal hassle of Dad's estate," she added. "And what's this about you only sleeping a few hours every night for the past few months? Kerry says you've been exhausted.''

"That couldn't be helped,'' Patrick asserted, his mouth set in a tight line.

"If I'd been here, all this could have been avoided.'' She shut her eyes briefly, then gave Patrick a determined look. "I want to get the business back on track again.''

"Then let's do it.''

Maggie's shoulders relaxed, and she realized she'd clenched her hands so hard, the nails had left indentations in her palms. "About this new guide,'' she prompted. "How much experience does he have?''

"Four years rafting in Oregon. He has a valid CPR certificate, and I've called his references. Carl's taking him out on the river today, and I thought you might check him out on a run next week. After Rawnick, I don't want any mistakes.''

"Good idea.'' Her eyes narrowed slightly. "There's something else we need to talk about. It seems Mark had another reason for being here this week besides camping. The BLM assigned him to investigate us, then—''

"What?'' Patrick interrupted.

Maggie took a deep breath. "He took himself off the case officially, but he's promised to help us turn things around.''

"You don't sound very convinced."

"I'm not. I don't trust my judgment when it comes to men. You know that."

"Sis, that was a long time ago. You're jumping to some pretty quick conclusions."

"Maybe." *And maybe not*, she added to herself.

Patrick's look turned thoughtful. "You know, Mark's in a good position to help us. He knows the BLM inside and out, and he knows the director too. Let's give it a shot."

"At least we can listen," she agreed warily. "No sense in turning down free advice." Something nagged at her, something she had wanted to ask Patrick about. Then she remembered what it was. "Have you been out back in the shed in the last few days?"

"Why? You planning on spring cleaning?"

"Hardly." She raised her brows. "But I stored the trash bags out there, the ones filled with the debris I picked up from the site. Just now, when I was looking for the hammer, it looked as if someone had gone through them."

"Not me, sis. Must be your imagination."

Taking a deep breath, she decided her imagination caused more trouble than she needed right now. Glancing at the stack of envelopes she'd placed on the counter, she made a face.

The gesture wasn't lost on Patrick. "Hand me

some of those. You never did like anything that kept you rooted in one spot.''

She sighed. ''You've got that right. I have to leave here by six. I showed up late for the last meeting, and I don't want to miss anything important.''

She made good time on the freeway. Fifty miles, fifty minutes, and the coalition meeting was about to start. Entering the building, she saw Gary standing on the far side of the room. He was talking to three other men and, by the serious set of their faces, the conversation seemed important. She decided not to interrupt.

A table stood along one wall of the room, with stacks of papers and pamphlets arranged in neat rows. She walked over and started reading a booklet detailing the highlights of the government's plan for the colossal dam.

Mark walked in behind Kay Rogers. She was an important member of the coalition, and he liked her well enough, but Kay had a tendency to put on airs—the femme fatale kind. He knew she didn't mean anything by it; she put on the charm school routine for any man between the ages of ten and ninety.

He just wondered why a woman with an MBA from Stanford, the owner of a graphics design business, acted so giddy. But then there was a lot he couldn't figure out about women. Probably never would.

"Mark—" Kay put a hand on his arm and pressed lightly. "I was just going to ask you. . . ." Her sugary voice trailed off, then she looked up and fluttered her lashes. "My father's having a dinner party at the ranch on Saturday evening. He thought you might want to come, maybe do some fund-raising. You know how keen he is on the coalition."

Mark pursed his lips. The thought of spending an entire evening with Kay and her father's wealthy social circle didn't sound like his kind of night.

"It's just a small gathering," she assured him. "Some of Daddy's friends. Clayborne Stewart, James and Victoria Hunt." She pressed one pearly-pink manicured nail to her lips. "Louis Martin and Mavis Durham."

A whistle escaped Mark's lips. "Quite a group. I've heard of Stewart. Doesn't he sit on the boards of quite a few banks in Sacramento?"

"Yes, but it's Mavis I want you to talk to. She's got loads of money and belongs to several environmental groups. Most of them are global. You know, saving the rainforests, that sort of thing. But I think she might be interested in what we're doing."

"You know the coalition inside and out, Kay. Why don't you ask for the contribution?"

"Because," Kay drawled, running her tongue over even white teeth, "Mavis is one of those older ladies who think only men have anything important to say." She pressed a hand on his arm again. "I'm sure she'd be more receptive if you asked. Besides, you're the head of the coalition—"

"Not officially," he interrupted, then folded his arms across his chest. "I don't know. I've got a project that'll keep me up near Sycamore Springs this weekend. I'd like to make these connections, but I may have to decline."

Kay opened the tiny red leather purse dangling from one shoulder and retrieved a scrap of paper and a pen. "Here's the address. Cocktails at seven, dinner at eight."

Mark tucked the slip of paper into his pocket. "I can't promise, Kay. This other project comes first."

Maggie stood in the corner, glancing over the edges of the leaflet, watching Kay fawn all over Mark. She frowned. *If that woman flutters her eyelashes one more time, I'm going to shut them permanently*, she fumed. Slamming the pamphlet down, she marched over.

"Hello, Mark. Kay." She smiled brightly at Mark, then turned toward Kay. The stab of jealousy had been unexpected, and she was more than a little confused about her feelings. Why should she care if Kay flirted with Mark? He'd betrayed her, hadn't he?

"Maggie!" Kay greeted her warmly. "Are you going to volunteer for one of my committees? We can sure use your help."

"I've been thinking about it, if I have the time," she answered. "Which committees did you have in mind?"

Kay shrugged. "Take your pick. They're all understaffed. There's publicity, advertising, environmental issues, research, and we have another we call 'Big Brother.' If you like dealing with the three-piece-suits from Washington, that's the ticket."

Mark cut in. "Maggie needs something substantive. How about environmental issues?"

Kay nodded. "That's a good choice. Maggie, what do you think about—"

Mark interrupted. "I'll leave you two to figure out which one is best. I have to get the meeting started."

Kay watched Mark walk toward the front of the room, then turned to Maggie and sighed. "He's quite a guy."

"You think so?" Maggie asked in a flat voice.

Kay took her arm. "Of course, silly. Everyone does. Brains and brawn—quite a package." She paused. "You know, I've been trying to get Mark interested in one of my girlfriends for ages."

"Really?" Maggie felt her throat go dry.

"Yes. It took a lot of doing, but I finally convinced him to go to a few cocktail parties." She inched closer, lowering her voice. "A gorgeous friend of mine practically flung herself at his feet. Gave him her home *and* car-phone numbers."

"Were they serious?"

"Serious? He never even called," she said in a horrified tone. "Finally *she* called him, and he made some excuse, said he was busy and would call in a week." She widened her eyes in astonishment. "Well he never did call. My friend was heartbroken and begged me to find out why. You'll never guess what he said."

Maggie couldn't stop herself from asking, "No, what?"

"That she wasn't the kind of woman he was looking for!" Kay said in a huff. "Men! I swear. Who knows what goes on in their heads?" Suddenly she brightened. "Come on, let's mingle. I'll introduce you around, then we'll talk."

"Okay," Maggie agreed hesitantly, wondering what she and Kay could possibly talk about. They weren't on the same wavelength; they weren't even in the same hemisphere.

A few minutes later, Gary rescued her by suggesting they find a seat. Mark was already behind the podium. ''The boss doesn't like to start late.'' Gary pointed to the clock on the wall.

''Boss?'' The word caught Maggie by surprise.

As they chose chairs and sat down, Gary leaned close and whispered, ''The coalition's been trying to hire him away from the BLM for a month now. Our grass roots organization has been in operation for six or seven months, but it's obvious we're going big-time. The government's already scheduled hearings, and there's a tremendous amount of work to do. We're backed by some of the wealthiest top-level private enterprises in Sacramento, and they want Mark full-time.''

Mark's voice boomed from the front of the room. ''If I could have your attention.'' The noise level in the room dropped to a whisper, then turned quiet. Mark stood with his legs spread apart, his hands locked behind his back. He had the air of a man in charge, one who gave orders and expected them to be followed.

''We have a lot of ground to cover tonight, but first I'd like to discuss another project. Although not part of coalition business, it deals with environmental issues and the Auburn River.'' He looked out over the audience and paused. ''It's something I believe we should be involved in.''

He moved from one side of the room to the other, talking as he paced. ''No point in discussing the whys and wherefores. In the final analysis, it's not important. But what *is* important is that some no-account person has trashed a dozen spots along the river. There's been some ecological damage.''

''What kind of damage?'' a man called out.

Mark leaned against the lectern. ''Nothing a dozen dedicated people can't fix. There's been some dumping, plants uprooted and destroyed, and,''—his voice turned sarcastic—''some unfortunate rearrangement of terrain.'' Mark stepped back and looked over the audience. ''I think we can wrap it up in one day if we get started at sunup. Anyone game for a little hard work for a good cause?''

Maggie stared at Mark, her mind reeling. What was he thinking, asking these people to help solve her problems? It had nothing to do with them or the coalition. She looked around the room as the whispering started, then grew louder.

Gary stood up. ''I've got Saturday free. We can use my truck.''

Another man stood. ''Kathy and I can go. We can fit a third in our truck if anyone needs a ride.''

Maggie brightened as several more hands were raised. This was really happening. He had simply asked, and they were saying yes. Mark had told her he'd take care of everything, and maybe he would, just like he'd promised.

Mark put his hands behind his back and nodded.

"Looks like we've got our volunteers. Kay, will you sign people up after the meeting?"

"Of course. I'll work out carpooling too."

Mark looked out over the audience. "Now. . . . " He leaned into the lectern. "Down to business."

Maggie glanced at the podium. Mark was talking about statistics and pointing to a graph set up behind him. She pursed her lips, realizing she'd lost her train of thought. She should be concentrating on the subject at hand, not daydreaming. If these people, these wonderful new friends she'd found, were willing to help her, she owed the coalition something in return. If they failed to stop the dam from being built, her outfitter days were over anyway. It seemed that her dreams and goals were tied up with theirs—and Mark's.

She turned to Kay, leaned close, and whispered, "I want to work on the environmental issues committee and help sign people up for Saturday."

Kay smiled and whispered behind her hand, "I'm so glad. We're outnumbered by men in this organization, and although I love the dears, we don't want them running the world, do we?"

Maggie slid a surprised look at Kay. There was obviously more to her than she'd first thought.

After the meeting ended, Maggie helped with the sign-up, thanking each person who volunteered. Then she noticed Mark standing to one side of the room, involved in an intense conversation with four men. He kept nodding his head, listening to one man in particular.

"I wonder what that's all about?" she asked Kay.

"The tall man and the one in the suit are two of our principal backers. The rest are heads of committees. They're trying to convince Mark to accept a position as director of the coalition. I think he's close, and tonight may clinch it."

"Why tonight?"

"We finally have enough money to offer him a decent salary. It's not as much as he's making now, but with Mark, money's not the first priority. That's what makes him different, and the right choice to lead the coalition." Kay opened a slim briefcase, tucking papers and pens inside. "That's about it. We've got ten people for Saturday, plus you and Mark. That's the dozen he asked for." She sighed and fluttered her lashes. "Mark's incredible."

"What do you mean?" Maggie asked warily.

Kay shrugged. "All he has to do is ask, and people volunteer. He's a born leader. I'm just glad he's on our side."

Mark walked up behind them. "How many people did we get?"

"An even dozen." Kay handed him the list. "I've got to run. Call me about Saturday night," she said, starting for the door. "See you, Maggie," she called out with a wave.

Maggie swiveled her head around, lips tight, her expression hard. She wondered who was doing the chasing, Mark or Kay. If it was Mark, then he was just like Todd. Words flashed through her mind. Don Juan. Playboy. She decided it was better that she'd found out now—her reaction to Mark's conversation with Kay told her she was headed for trouble.

"Can I walk you out?" Mark touched her arm lightly. He hadn't missed the fierce look on her face when Kay mentioned Saturday night. It proved she cared, although she was doing her best to look nonchalant and uninterested. "What's your hurry?" He lengthened his stride and caught up with her.

"I have to get home," she insisted, then stopped in her tracks and shook her head. "I'm sorry. You went to a lot of trouble organizing the cleanup operation, and I haven't even thanked you—for tonight and for Saturday."

"You know I want to help," Mark said.

"Yes," she said. "I do. I wish Patrick could be there too, but I don't see how he can," she said apologetically. "There's the store, and he doesn't want to be far from a telephone in case Kerry needs him."

"That's understandable. I talked to Patrick earlier today about Jake Rawnick, and he said he'd be working at Outdoor Odyssey both Saturday and Sunday."

"Did you get all the information you needed?" she asked.

"As much as Patrick knows, which isn't a lot. Apparently most of what Rawnick told him doesn't add up."

Maggie grimaced. "Yes, I know. Patrick's very trusting and believes in giving people the benefit of the doubt, but this time we got the short end of the stick."

"It's not over yet, Maggie. Henderson's already working on his report, and I plan to invite myself along when he meets with the director."

She shot him a speculative look. "At least you'll have something positive to add."

"Absolutely. It'll strengthen your position when Henderson tells Bingham about the cleanup operation. Listen, I thought we might send part of the group down in your rafts. You can see a lot from the water that you miss by hiking."

"Good idea. What can I do?"

"We need seedlings, plants, as many shovels, rakes, trowels, and plastic bags as you can find, and lunch for twelve."

"You've got it," she promised.

Just then they reached her car. Mark opened

the door for her, she threw her purse in, and she slid across the seat.

He leaned against the car door, his head inches from hers. "Do you have to leave so soon?" he asked. "I'd like to spend more time together."

Chapter Seven

Maggie realized she was staring out the front window instead of answering—that was how much Mark unnerved her—but she found herself unable to answer. She swallowed hard, then turned to look at Mark. There was no way around it; she didn't trust herself to be alone with him. Her feelings were too close to the surface. "Tonight's not a good night," she said, her voice hoarse.

He stared at her until he could tell from the way she blinked that he was making her nervous. He wanted to be with her, but she wasn't making it easy on him. She was turning it into a campaign. He stared at her a few seconds longer, then said, "You're a hard woman, Maggie Macguire."

"I'm as hard as I have to be," she said, resting an elbow on the open window, forcing him to pull back a few inches.

He opened his hands wide. "Are you sure? A cup of coffee doesn't take long."

She thought about telling him how she felt, how they had different agendas. His was here and now. Hers meant forever. But that would mean telling him that she cared, and that meant getting hurt. She couldn't risk that—not again.

"It's late, Mark," she whispered. "I have to get home."

He backed away from the car. "If that's what you want," he said, clearly disappointed.

She turned the key in the ignition, flipped on her headlights, and pulled out of the parking lot. She allowed herself one quick glance in the rear-view mirror. He stood there, arms folded across his chest, watching her drive away. A warning voice whispered in her head, and Maggie knew if she wasn't careful, he would be her undoing.

Mark watched her drive away. She was tough, all right. Hardheaded, stubborn, overly proud . . . exciting, wonderful, the kind of woman he wanted to get to know better, one who kept him slightly off balance and very interested. There were a lot of things he didn't know about Maggie, but one thing was certain. She intrigued him, and if he had to throw her over one shoulder, cart her off, and force her to sit still for an hour or two while he explained things to her, so be it.

He looked around the dark, deserted parking

lot, then stared up at the moon. It was almost full and yellow like molten gold. He walked slowly toward his Ranger, suddenly realizing he was very lonely.

"You've got enough food here to feed an army," Mark called out to Maggie before sliding another ice chest in the back of the Ranger. At least she was in a better mood than the last time he'd seen her. He shook his head. Women. He still couldn't figure out what had gone wrong on Monday night. He didn't understand women, no matter how hard he tried. That's one reason why he wasn't married and probably never would be.

He glanced around to see Maggie carting still another wicker basket over to him. "Here, let me take that." He lengthened his stride to take the heavy basket from her. "You must've gotten up before dawn to get this ready. It's only seven now."

"It's the least I could do," she answered. "But I still think you should've told everybody the whole story."

"I didn't see the point. They're helping because they care about the environment and because they're good people."

"I know, but I feel guilty."

He reached out and touched her lightly on the arm. "Forget it. Pay them back by supporting the coalition. I'm not above bribery to get another member.''

''You don't have to bribe me. I have every intention of joining.'' She checked the baskets, coolers, and equipment that filled the back of the Ranger.

Gary walked up behind them. ''We're ready to go. I've got one trailer hitched up, and Toby's got the other. We can get the rafts and equipment set up by the time everyone else gets there.''

''Then let's get a move on.'' Mark glanced at his watch. ''It'll take twenty minutes to get to the river, another thirty to inflate the rafts and load everything.'' He looked at Gary. ''Right on schedule.''

''Boss, we all know about your schedules and how irritable you get when things don't go according to plan.''

Mark pretended to glower at him. He was constantly ribbed for his timekeeping, but it got the job done. ''Yeah, yeah,'' he said jokingly. ''If you're not careful, pal, I'll put you in charge.''

Gary laughed and gave him a look of horror. ''Not on your life.'' He waved at Toby. ''Let's follow the boss.''

Mark turned to Maggie. ''I guess you're riding with me, if that's all right.''

Maggie smiled her approval, and they left Sycamore Springs and spun onto the highway in less than five minutes. Mark slipped a cassette into the tape deck. "How about some Jerry Lee Lewis?" he said, singing the opening bars along with the Killer as they headed down the highway.

"Do you always listen to fifties music?" she asked, raising her voice over the thump-thump of the bass.

He turned down the volume. " 'Great Balls of Fire' is a classic. Jerry Lee was a genius! The Big Bopper, Elvis . . . the music today doesn't compare."

"Maybe, but I like mine a little quieter, more classical."

He put his arm out the window and hooked it on top of the door. "How about coming by the house and letting me change your mind about oldies? I've got some great sounds."

When Maggie didn't answer, he gave an exasperated sigh. "You know, my friends *do* come over and listen to music. We are *friends,* aren't we, Maggie?" He turned and eyed her curiously.

Realizing she wished there could be more between them made it difficult to answer, but after a moment's silence she said, "Of course, and I'd love to listen to some of your music."

Mark reached over and gently touched her hand, then held on tight. "Good. I'll give you a call just as soon as I know my schedule next week."

"Here we are," he announced a few minutes later, pulling off onto a narrow dirt road. A cloud of dust blew up from under the Ranger's wheels and Maggie fanned the air in front of her. She got out of the car as Gary and Toby pulled in behind them.

"Hi, guys," she greeted them.

"Hello, yourself," Gary answered. "So where is everybody? This is a pretty small work crew."

"I'm sure the others will be along," Mark said. "Let's get started." They inflated both rafts with the portable hydraulic pump and were looking over the life jackets when he checked his watch. "Late," he announced with a frown. "Fifteen minutes."

"You worry too much. You'll get an ulcer," Gary told him with a barely disguised chortle. "They'll be here."

A few minutes later, two cars turned onto the dirt road, followed quickly by a third. Maggie felt the dust and heat rise. It was going to be a scorcher. Already at least seventy-five, it would probably reach ninety by mid afternoon.

"You found three sites?" Maggie asked one of the volunteers as she wrapped up leftovers. They'd just finished lunch, and a quick look at her watch told her it was after two.

"Yeah." He nodded. "The hikers hit three and I guess you rafters cleared up four more."

"I still can't believe it." She shook her head. "It's all done. Finished."

Mark walked over, a cup in one hand. "It's been a good day." He downed the lemonade and ran the back of his hand over his mouth. "The only hard part was moving all those rocks back to the river's edge up by Goodyear's Bar. Why anyone would build a fire pit six feet across is a mystery to me, but it was an invitation for a bonfire and we don't need any fire hazards."

Gary joined them. "Mother Earth is back to her natural, pristine self—after a little help from her friends."

Mark slapped Gary on the back, then turned to Maggie. "How about giving these volunteers a run down some white water?"

"Sounds good. There's some Class II+ up ahead. Nothing dangerous, just some fun. We've got room for all of us if we sit close."

"Right up my alley." Mark turned to the group and called out, "Anybody who wants to raft— come on."

It came as no surprise when the air resounded with whoops and shouts and a dozen pairs of hands grabbed life jackets and paddles.

"Mark, why don't you pilot the other raft?" Maggie suggested, picking up a jacket.

"Let me help you," he said, moving in front of her.

"I don't need any—"

"I know," he interrupted. "You don't need help." He placed a hand on either side of the jacket, forcing her to meet his gaze. "But I'm going to anyway."

She stood there while he secured the clasps on the jacket. He was taking too long, and she suspected it was on purpose. Glancing around, she realized people were watching. She detected a few sly smiles, then said, "Mark, this is embarrassing."

"Why?" He cocked his head to one side, pretending to recheck the fastenings. Before she could stop him, he pulled up on both sides of the jacket, forcing her to stand on tiptoe, then leaned down and brushed his lips across hers.

"Because people are watching," she said.

"I don't mind," he teased, loosening his hold and stepping back.

Her mouth dropped. "You're impossible."

He gave her a wicked grin. "Maggie, my darling, you don't know the half of it."

She perched her hands on her hips and gave him a look designed to wilt any man. That was the problem. She *did* know the half of it. He was so typically male, it was ridiculous.

He shook his head and gave her a wink. "You're cute when you're angry."

"Let's raft," she said between tight lips. Whirling around, she grabbed the lead rope of one raft. "Come on, whoever's going." She eyed Mark. "Our leader is piloting the other raft, so choose up sides and let's go."

Two bright yellow rafts plied the waters of the Auburn, vying for lead position. Mark's raft surged ahead, but Maggie urged her crew on until they were neck and neck.

"Come on, pull," she told her crew, dipping her paddle deep into the current, straining to pull ahead. "Get the lead out!" Their raft inched ahead of Mark's as her team matched her stroke for stroke.

Mark let out a sharp whistle. "Let's go! We can't let them beat us."

Paddling furiously, Maggie chanced a look at Mark. His competitive edge showed in the way his legs were planted on either side of the raft. He'd passed on the idea of using toeholds. Of course, so had she. The rapids weren't dangerous here. They were fun. He had a steely look of determination about him. Then she saw the smile spread across his tanned face and the broad wink he gave her.

She laughed. He might be competitive, but he liked having fun too. Well, she intended to give him a run for his money. Losing went against everything her father had taught her. The only thing she knew was to give it one heck of a shot. That's how she did everything. Full-out, top-speed, no-holds-barred.

She narrowed her eyes. "Come on, let's go," she urged her crew. "They're gaining on us."

They were coming into a wide section of the river where a lively series of rapids stretched out in front of them like the tracks of a dippy roller coaster. Both rafts entered at the same time. They ran the rapids neck and neck, the rafts so close that paddles kept getting tangled up as they bumped and jostled against each other. When the rapids calmed, they resorted to a boisterous water fight, splashing and spraying water until both sides begged for mercy.

"We might as well go swimming," Maggie suggested, ducking from still another spray of water Mark aimed in her direction.

"Great idea," he agreed, then jumped in the river and started maneuvering the rafts to one side. Gary joined him, and they quickly tied the lead ropes around some sturdy bushes growing close to the river's edge.

Maggie stood up, tugged the soggy cutoffs she wore over her bathing suit down to her ankles, and tossed them aside. Then she took a deep breath and dove into the river. When she surfaced, she blinked hard and slicked back her hair with both hands. The water felt cool and wonderful. She watched everyone scramble overboard and Mark dive into the water, coming up next to her a few seconds later.

"Whew!" he yelled out, whipping his hair back. "This is great!" He squinted up into the sun, water streaming off his face, and he laughed. "What a great idea."

She grinned back at him. "I'll second that."

The dim sound of splashes reverberating in her ears grew louder and she looked over to see Gary, Toby, and Allen start to spray them with a deluge of water. She shrieked as Mark let out a loud war whoop and lunged at his friends.

It had been a long day on the river, but they'd finished everything. Mark knew tomorrow would be even longer—he'd promised to help Gary move into his new apartment, and he wanted to talk to Henderson. He glanced at his watch. It was after six. If he left Sycamore Springs now, he'd have time to call Henderson before hitting the sheets, but he'd never make Kay's cocktail party. He'd have to call and cancel.

Then he glanced over at Maggie. They'd just finished unloading all the equipment in Outdoor Odyssey's parking lot. She stood by Gary's truck, talking to Kathy and Allen.

He swallowed hard, ignoring the feeling of tenderness that washed over him. Those emotions had started the night in the parking lot after the first coalition meeting, and they seemed to get stronger every time he looked at her. He might as well stop fighting the inevitable—he wasn't going anywhere. He'd call Frank tomorrow. He ambled over to the truck and overheard Allen commenting to Kathy, "If we're going to pick up the kids before dinnertime, we better hit the road."

"You have children?" Maggie asked.

Kathy chuckled and held up four fingers.

"Four?" Maggie grinned in surprise. "I'd like a family one day, but how on earth do you manage?"

"Simple," Kathy answered with a nonchalant shrug. "We're into outdoors things. Camping, fishing, baseball, soccer. A calendar on the fridge tells everybody what's happening every day and"—she smiled up at her husband—"Allen's great. He does his share."

"I'd like another baby," Allen said, putting his arm around Kathy's shoulder. "But the wife says four's enough."

Mark laughed, a flustered, uneasy sound. "One rug rat's enough for anybody," he said cynically.

Kathy gave her husband a broad smile. "I don't know. Maybe when the youngest rug rat starts school, we'll be ready for another." She stood on tiptoe and kissed Allen.

Mark couldn't figure it out. Kathy and Allen had been married almost ten years, they had four noisy, rambunctious kids, and they still acted as if they were in love. He found it almost embarrassing. They were a new-age version of "Ozzie and Harriet," and as far from reality as he could imagine. Families just didn't come like that anymore.

He knew the divorce rates and had grown up with his emotions divided between two parents he loved but who couldn't seem to stay together. He didn't see why people bothered to try when the odds were against any couple seeing their fifth anniversary. It was all too painful, especially when children were involved.

After Kathy and Allen had driven away, Maggie turned to him. "Thirsty? There's beer in the fridge."

Mark ran the back of his hand over his forehead. "Sounds great. Evening's almost here and it's still hot."

"Come on, then. We've got fan power inside."

Maggie went to the tiny refrigerator her father had built in under one counter and brought out two bottles. Mark gulped down half the bottle before setting it on the counter, then ran a tongue over his lips. "I hate for the day to end. How about dinner tonight?'' He reached for her hand, threading his fingers between hers.

''Tonight? The church social's tonight.''

''You have church socials?''

''Sure. Every other week.''

He wondered what a social was like. He'd never been to one. His family wasn't religious, and he'd always been curious. He'd taken a religion class in college, but it had taken a historical perspective. He'd been more interested in the feeling of belonging that he'd sensed from watching families go to church on Sunday mornings. When he was a kid, he'd watch them through his bedroom window, the boys in suits with their hair slicked back and combed, the girls looking like princesses.

He'd always been intrigued by families because his own had been divided by divorce. He knew it was the desire to belong, rather than the religion, that drew him. And after all these years, he still thought theology was interesting.

''Socials aren't very exciting,'' Maggie said unconvincingly. ''Potluck, fruit punch, little kids running around.'' She wrinkled her nose. ''You wouldn't like it—all those rug rats.''

''Oh yeah?'' he said, rising to the challenge he heard in her voice. ''It sounds like fun. I think I'll tag along—if you don't mind.''

She took a long drink of beer before answering nonchalantly, ''Suit yourself.''

"Mind if I use your phone?" he asked.

"Go ahead."

He dialed a number and waited. "Kay? It's Mark."

Maggie felt a stab of jealousy, one she didn't like. He was using her phone to call Kay.

"Fine, fine. The project went well. Listen, about tonight. . . . "

Maggie's lip curled. She had no intention of standing there and listening to Mark's conversation with Kay. Starting across the room, she heard his laugh and stopped. It sounded like a response to someone amusing, someone who flirted and made a man feel special, someone cute and blond, very blond.

She narrowed her eyes, took a big breath, and blew at her bangs. So he was into games, was he? Well, she didn't intend to take the bait. She made her way across the room and went outside, hoping the sun would brighten her disposition. Mark certainly hadn't.

"Kay, about tonight," Mark said into the receiver. "I can't make it. I'm staying in Sycamore Springs later than I thought."

"Maggie, I really enjoyed the social," Mark said enthusiastically as they walked up the darkened steps to her front door. "Everybody was so friendly and . . . the kids.'' He shook his head. ''There must have been thirty.''

''I warned you.''

''But that's what made it so special. Growing up with no brothers and sisters, I missed being with kids.''

She laughed, remembering how he'd been fascinated by the children. It was as if he'd never been around any before. The first hour had been kind of tense, but after a two-year-old climbed uninvited into Mark's lap, he loosened up, even playing patty cake with the toddler until Maggie rescued him.

''You made up for lost time tonight,'' she said.

''I especially liked Father O'Reilly. Quite an interesting man.'' He checked his watch. ''As much as I hate to, I'd better go. It's almost eleven and I've still got a long drive.''

He felt her touch his arm gently.

''Mark, I can't thank you enough for all your help today. Getting your friends to help clean up the river. It's beautiful again.''

''No big deal.'' He shrugged. ''I hope it'll make a difference at the hearing. I called Henderson from the church while you were helping to refill the punch bowl. He files his report early next week, and the hearing's set for Friday at ten. You'll get an official notice in the mail. The letter went out yesterday. Once he finds out you've corrected all the problems, Bingham may let you off with a warning.''

''You think it'll be okay?''

He took a deep breath. ''We'll see, but Bingham's new at the job and still trying to impress the big guys. I don't see what he'd gain by revoking your permit. Your family has had it so long, there could be some backlash from the other outfitters, and that could cause problems upstairs.''

''True, but would he care?''

Mark pursed his lips. ''Good question. I guess we'll find out on Monday. I wish I could be there, but since Henderson's the investigator, there's no valid reason for me to attend.''

Maggie nodded, her expression grim.

She watched him drive away, went inside, closed the door, and leaned against it. She desperately needed time to think, time to sort out her feelings. She felt a surge in her heart and closed her eyes. Her mind replayed the evening's events. *Sometimes you think you know someone, and then you find out there's a lot more beneath the surface,* she thought. Tonight she'd discovered that about Mark. It went a long way toward convincing her that he wasn't like Todd. If only she could be sure.

Kerry sat on the couch in the living room, a book perched on her abdomen. She looked up, then put a bookmark at the page.

"Still awake?" Maggie asked.

"I'm just going up. How was your evening?"

Maggie closed her eyes, remembering the whispers and twittering she'd overheard when people thought she wasn't looking. She'd expected that. It was flattering being with Mark. All the unmarried women had been green with envy, and he'd made friends with everyone.

"I had a great time. Mark's a born socializer. By the time we left, he'd met everybody. He even played tag with some kids."

"Fit right in, did he?"

Maggie nodded. "Funny. Almost as if he'd been there before. He and Father O'Reilly spent a lot of time together." Maggie could still hear the words reverberating in her head. She just couldn't believe them. "Mark told Father O'Reilly he wanted to join the weekly discussion group."

Kerry's mouth dropped. "Take instruction in the church?"

"No. He didn't say anything about that, but I don't think he's ever talked to a pastor before. I introduced them, and the next thing I knew, they were talking theology." She threw her hands in the air. "Mark had some pretty definite ideas about faith, and lots of questions too. He wanted Father O'Reilly's opinions."

"But that's wonderful."

"Kerry, I'm not so sure. He'll be coming to town all the time."

"And what's wrong with that, I'd like to know?"

Maggie sat on the couch, picked up a needle-point cushion, one of a dozen Kerry had made, and hugged it to her. She knew what was wrong. She was in love with Mark, but he wasn't in love with her. She wanted commitment. Mark had made it pretty clear that he didn't want a wife and children.

Kerry gave her an exasperated look. "I've heard you go on about the kind of man you want. Intelligent, adventurous, full of curiosity. . . ." She pursed her lips together and thought for a second. "Let's see. You also mentioned tall and handsome. Right?"

Maggie bit down on her lip. Now that she heard the words, they sounded immature, even ridiculous. "Yes, but—"

"No 'buts' about it. You write your recipe for husband material and what happens? One walks in. Bold as brass." She wagged her finger. "How much better do you think they come than Mark?"

Chapter Eight

On Friday morning, Maggie and Patrick followed Frank Henderson down the long, narrow hallway on their way to the office where the director would decide their fate. This was it. D day. Their Waterloo.

For the tenth time, she thought about how the week had dragged on. She hadn't seen Mark since Saturday night. Kerry's baby was overdue, and she'd been afraid to risk the drive to Sacramento. Neither she nor Patrick wanted to be anywhere but home, but they'd had no choice today. The letter from the BLM had come registered mail, return receipt requested, on embossed United States government stationery, looking very official.

Their next-door neighbor, Evelyn, had offered to stay with Kerry until they returned, but both

Patrick and Maggie were nervous about being fifty miles away.

At least it would finally be over. They would have a decision on their permit. After all Mark's assurances, they hadn't been too worried, but Frank Henderson had seemed cold and aloof when they'd met. Maggie dug her hand into the pocket of her beige pleated trousers and crossed her fingers.

Henderson knocked on Bingham's door, then opened it. The director sat slouched behind his desk, glasses perched on the end of his nose. They walked in. "Tom Bingham," Henderson said, "Patrick and Maggie Macguire."

Bingham shook hands, then waved at two chairs positioned in front of his desk. "Please, sit down," he said, settling himself back in his chair while Henderson chose a straight-backed one nearby.

The director hunched forward, resting his elbows on the big mahogany desk. "Just a few preliminaries and we'll get started." He cleared his throat. "Although this meeting may seem informal, as director of the Bureau of Land Management, I head up the governmental agency that regulates outfitters who operate on government land." He gave them an impersonal smile. "Outfitters such as yourselves. I intend to make a final determination on the status of your rafting permit today.''

Bingham picked up Henderson's report, scanned the first page, then looked at Patrick over his glasses. ''I've read all the details of how you inherited the permit from your father. I understand Ms. Macguire has been out of the country for some time. Left the running of the business''—he looked back at the report—''two businesses to Mr. Macguire. Is that right?''

''Yes,'' Maggie confirmed. ''I was fulfilling a two-year commitment with the Peace Corps.''

Bingham nodded. ''I see.'' He turned to Maggie. ''The Peace Corps is a most admirable undertaking, Ms. Macguire, but under the circumstances, I'll direct my questions to Mr. Macguire. He appears to be more familiar with the matter at hand.''

He tapped his fingers on his desk and pursed his lips. ''Mr. Macguire, why don't you give me some background information?''

Patrick cleared his throat. ''I hired Jake Rawnick to help me run the businesses. After a few weeks, I noticed some problems.''

Bingham turned to Henderson. ''When did we receive the first complaint?''

''Second week in April,'' Henderson answered. ''A couple from San Francisco complained about a guide using foul language, acting rude, and not giving any safety instructions.''

Bingham turned back to Patrick. ''After you got our letter about the complaints, what action did you take?''

''I called Jake on it. He said he'd gotten angry because the woman had lost an oar.'' Patrick tightened his lips. ''I accepted his explanation. Oars are expensive.''

Bingham frowned. ''And what about the lack of safety instructions?''

''Rawnick disputed it. He said he'd followed everything to the letter. I gave him the benefit of the doubt. I figure everyone deserves that, and he came with good references. Of course, later I found out they were all lies, but at the time''— Patrick threw up his hands—''I believed him.''

Maggie grimaced, then leaned back in her chair and angled one leg over her knee. She didn't like the way this was going. She turned to Patrick. ''But you started watching Rawnick, didn't you? Watching his behavior?''

''Not then, no. Not until the second letter.''

Maggie closed her eyes, then opened them again. Patrick hadn't taken the hint. They were dead.

Bingham leaned forward. ''So you didn't consider the first warning serious?''

"No. It wasn't like that. It's just that I gave him a second chance."

Bingham waved an impatient hand in the air. "Did anyone mention his drinking on the job?"

"The last call I got. Then I fired him."

"And what about all this damage to your put-in sites along the river? I note there were a dozen places mentioned in this report."

Maggie broke in. "Mr. Bingham, we've gone to each of our sites, checked over our entire route, carried trash out, and landscaped large areas. I think we've found everything. There's been no lasting damage. We've gone to great lengths to—"

Bingham snorted, his face turning red. "It'll take a long time for nature to repair the damage detailed in this report. Your employee was careless and irresponsible. I applaud your efforts, Ms. Macguire, but we've got another serious matter to consider." His eyes narrowed and he slammed one hand on the desk. "Did you know anything about this firearm?"

Maggie swallowed hard. Looking at Bingham, she saw all their hopes slide into oblivion. Patrick had told her about the gun while driving to Sacramento that morning. Mark had apparently discussed it with him earlier, but Patrick had kept it to himself. He said worrying about it wouldn't change what had happened.

"No, I didn't know about it then. I found out recently, when Mark Wilde called and asked me about it."

The director's face turned grim. "What's Wilde got to do with this?" he asked Henderson. "I thought he was off the case."

"He is," Henderson answered. "But—"

Maggie interrupted. She had to get the director's attention away from Mark. "Look, Mr. Bingham," she insisted tersely. "We didn't know anything about the gun. What kind of people do you take us for?"

Bingham frowned. "That's exactly what I'm trying to find out, Ms. Macguire." He paused, then went on. "And you say you knew nothing about it? You didn't have a clue that he carried the gun on the rafts when he worked for you?"

Patrick shook his head sharply.

"When he transported your customers?"

"No, sir," Patrick answered vehemently.

Bingham leaned back in his chair. "Earlier this morning, Mr. Henderson called several complainants and asked about the gun." He gestured toward Henderson. "Tell them about the conversation with Mrs. Wilson."

Henderson retrieved a small notepad from his shirt pocket and cleared his throat. "Jeannette Wilson says she saw a small pistol in one of the dry bags when they stopped for lunch."

"That proves it was Rawnick," Maggie declared, inching up in her chair.

Henderson broke in. "Mrs. Wilson said there were two guides the day she went down the river. The other guide's name was Carl."

Patrick's response was vehement. "Carl's been a friend of my father's, and ours, for twenty years. It certainly couldn't have been him. That's impossible!"

"Absolutely," Maggie echoed. "There's no way." Her cheeks burned with anger. She wouldn't stand by and see Carl accused. Her own godfather!

Bingham tapped his fingers together, then opened his hands. "You can see my predicament. You say it's one employee; Mrs. Wilson has given an eyewitness account mentioning another. I'm not in a position to give you the benefit of the doubt. Mrs. Wilson's statement only strengthens the bureau's case for mismanagement. Of course. . . . " He tapped his fingers together again. "There *is* the lighter." He turned to Henderson. "You verified the birth date?"

"Yes," he confirmed. "From Mr. Macguire's employment records. It does point the finger at Rawnick."

Bingham shrugged. "But there's no proof. Too bad Mr. Rawnick never surfaced." The director gave Patrick and Maggie a hard stare. "Regulations prohibit firearms on the river. I have no choice but to hold you responsible for your employee, whichever one it was.''

Maggie took a deep breath. They were doomed. There was no question about it.

Bingham cleared his throat. ''There are a dozen outfitters who've waited years for a permit to run the Auburn. As you know, new permits are no longer issued. The only way to acquire one is through a lottery system when a company goes out of business or loses theirs. I'm revoking this one,'' he announced firmly. ''Effective immediately.''

Maggie gasped, then stood up. ''You can't!''

''I'm sorry, Ms. Macguire, but I have no other choice.''

''Is there anything we can do?''

Henderson broke in. ''If Rawnick comes forward and admits his guilt, there's provision for appeal.''

Bingham nodded. ''Mr. Henderson's correct. You could file an appeal.''

Maggie's eyes grew huge. ''Rawnick. Jake Rawnick,'' she whispered hoarsely, then flew out the door and down the hall. She was almost to the front door of the building when Patrick caught up.

''Wait a minute, sis. I want to see Mark before we leave.''

"What for?"

"He wanted to know how it went. Besides, maybe he can help us find Rawnick."

Maggie bit down on her lower lip. As much as she wanted to, they couldn't involve Mark. "We can't, Patrick. You saw Bingham's reaction when his name was mentioned. He'll lose his job. We'll handle this ourselves."

Maggie slammed the receiver back in the cradle. "I've been on the phone since three o'clock and gotten nowhere," she told Patrick. "I know he's in the area; everything we've found points to it." She tapped her pencil on the desk. "I just don't know where."

"I wonder why he's stayed around."

"The only thing I've come up with is that he has some drinking cronies in Sacramento. Apparently he's floated around the area for years." She tapped her pencil again. "What if we had an artist draw a sketch of him? We could have a poster made up, you know, and offer a reward for information."

"Not a bad idea," Patrick agreed. "We haven't come up with anything better."

"Let's go over Rawnick's description again."

Patrick stretched, then answered, "Like I told you—mid thirties, sandy hair, medium complexion, stocky build."

"You could be describing a hundred guys," Maggie protested. "Surely there's something that made him stand out. How would I recognize him if I saw him on the street?"

Patrick folded his arms across his chest and closed his eyes. "He usually wore jeans or khaki pants and a cotton shirt."

She took a deep breath. "That narrows it down to every other man who lives in Sycamore Springs."

Patrick stared at the ceiling for a minute. "He had a funny walk. He leaned forward, so his head arched in front of him. His nose was a tad large and his eyes were close set. A strange color too. Pale green."

An image flashed before Maggie's eyes—a man walking away from her with a funny gait. "Patrick, I've seen him!"

"What?"

"He's here. I tell you, I've seen him in town. A few days ago I talked to a man across the street. I remember the eyes, and his walk seemed odd."

"It could be a coincidence. A lot of people have green eyes," Patrick said.

"Were his eyebrows full and wiry? This man had—"

Patrick grabbed her arm. "That's him! Come on. Maybe we can find him." He glanced at his watch. "It's five o'clock. He's a drinker. Let's check the taverns."

There were only four in town, including the bar in the hotel. As they left the last one, a small, dingy place next to the freeway, Maggie turned to Patrick. "I tell you, that bartender knows something."

"Yeah." Patrick shook his head. "I thought the guy at the end of the bar seemed pretty interested in our questions too."

"I don't know what more to do," Maggie said, the gravel on the parking lot making a crunching noise under her sneakers. "We can't *make* them tell us anything." She opened the driver's door of the car and got in. "Can we go to the police?"

Patrick eased into the passenger seat. "We can't prove he's done anything illegal. That's the problem."

She cranked the engine, pulled out of the parking lot, and started back to town. A second later, she squinted into the rearview mirror. A car had pulled on to the road behind them. Its headlights were on bright, the reflection nearly blinding her. She flipped up the rearview mirror, shadowing the light shining in her eyes. A minute later the other car's headlights dimmed, and Maggie readjusted the mirror.

"Let's stop at the store for a minute," Patrick

said as they drove onto the main street. "I want to pick up the ledgers and work on them at home."

"Did you call Kerry before we left?"

"No, but she knew I had to work on the accounts. Probably thinks I'm still at it."

She pulled into the parking lot of Outdoor Odyssey and cut the engine. "I'm going out back to check the storeroom again."

"Still looking for that matchbook?"

"Yes. I found it at the first site." She shrugged. "It may give us a lead."

She went around back and unlocked the door of the wooden shed, switched on the one small light, and scanned the room. Even though the door had been locked, someone had obviously been through the bags, and several were open. She went over to the cabinet, checking all the shelves.

"It isn't there," a gruff voice said.

She whirled around.

"I took the liberty of retrieving my stuff that you hid in there," Jake Rawnick said, closing the door behind him.

"What are you doing here?" Her voice scratched like sandpaper across her vocal chords.

"Well, now. I hear you're looking for me, running your mouth off to my friends and saying things about me I don't much like. Thought I'd come by so we could settle this. Just between us." A thin smile stretched across his face.

She felt the hairs on the back of her neck stand up as fear crept through her. Patrick wouldn't miss her for another five minutes. Maybe if she talked to him calmly, rationally, he would listen or leave. She took a deep breath and ran her tongue over suddenly dry lips.

"We can settle it," she told him. "You tell the BLM what you did, admit we knew nothing about you carrying a gun—"

"You mean this little old thing?" Rawnick reached behind his back and brought out a pistol from the waistband of his pants.

Her heart stopped, then started again.

"Ain't no law against having a gun in this state. I've even got a permit."

She swallowed hard and tried to stay calm. "Then you won't mind telling the BLM about it."

He held the gun in front of him, aimed it at the ceiling, and moved it to one side of the room, then the other. "Nah, I don't want to talk to them." He shrugged. "I got no reason to."

"It would help us out of a jam."

He cocked the gun, moving it slowly around the room again. "Now why would I want to help you? You know, I don't much appreciate the way your brother fired me. He's just like all the rest. He thinks 'cause he's the boss he can push a guy around." He brought the gun back to his side.

"Nobody's going to push me around no more." Rawnick held the gun out and looked at it. "Just because of a little fun on my part. Heck, a man's got to have some fun."

"It's a nice gun," she said, her voice breaking. She took a step forward and reached out her hand. She had to get the gun away from him. "Can I look at it?"

The door opened and Rawnick jumped at her, grabbing her around the waist, then yanking her around in front of him and aiming for the door.

Pinned against his chest, the air knocked out of her, she fought back as best she could. Pulling at his arm, she tried to break his grip. She couldn't.

Patrick put his hands in the air and stepped backward. "Wait a minute. Hold on. Jake, what's this all about?"

"Nothing. Nothing at all, except for you." He swore.

Maggie felt the gun in her ribs, poking through her shirt.

"Jake, put the gun down," Patrick said in a firm voice.

"Get back! Get outta here!" Rawnick demanded.

"All right. But let my sister go. She had nothing to do with this. Why don't we sit down and talk this over, just you and me?"

"You been talking too much already," Jake yelled hoarsely, then swore again. "Talking about me and asking questions. I didn't do nothing wrong. Just used some dumb animals for target practice. Didn't hurt nobody."

"That's right, Jake. And you don't want to hurt anybody now either." Patrick slowly extended one hand. "Give me the gun."

Rawnick looked at Maggie. "I'm not gonna hurt her. She's just goin' for a little ride with me. Wanted to look at my gun." He let out a loud, raucous cackle. "And I'm going to show it to her."

"Let me go," Maggie demanded, trying to jab him in the ribs. He just pulled tighter, so tight she could feel his fingers digging into her flesh.

Rawnick pulled her toward the door. "Out of the way!" he shouted, waving the gun in the air. "Over there!"

Slowly Patrick moved across the room, his eyes focused on Rawnick.

"Your sister's gonna help make up for the trouble you caused. I figure you owe me!" he wheezed loudly.

Maggie struggled as he dragged her toward the door. She tried to tangle her legs in his and make him fall, but he just kicked at her.

"I got me a little wildcat," Rawnick said with a leer. "I know how to take care of you, lady."

His shrill laugh ricocheted off the walls as he butted his shoulder against the door.

When it opened, two arms grabbed Rawnick from behind, forcing him to loosen his hold on Maggie. She recognized Mark just before she hit the ground, the same time the gun went off.

Maggie felt an explosion against her side, then pain as the bullet ripped through her. Blood, hot and thick, trickled, then ran down her front. She didn't hear the fight, the shouts, or the sound of the second bullet or the third.

She clutched her chest and watched the blood seep through her hands, covering her shirt with a massive red stain. Gulping for air, the last thing she saw was Mark and Rawnick grappling for the gun. Then she entered a sharp black void filled with pain.

"You need a doctor, Mr. Wilde."

"I can wait." Mark felt a numbing panic deep down in his gut, and it was taking over.

"You aren't doing her any good by being obstinate. Do you want to bleed all over the waiting room?" The technician put both hands on Mark's chest and forcibly pushed him down on the chair.

Young and heavyset, he wore a serious expression on his face. He'd just spent twelve hours on an emergency room shift and had been looking forward to going home to a hot bath and sleep.

"Get Dr. Zachery over here." He waved at a nurse around the corner in the emergency room.

"Just tell me how she is," Mark demanded. "She's been in there for an hour."

"They're wheeling her into surgery now."

"Surgery?"

"The bullet's lodged in her chest. They have to get it out. She's lost a lot of blood, but John Braverman's the best surgeon in the hospital."

"I want to see her." Mark stood toe-to-toe with the technician and glowered at him. "Tell me where she is."

"Mr. Wilde, I can't—"

"I said, tell me where she is." He poked the technician in the chest. "Otherwise I'll have to find her myself."

Mark heard his name and swiveled around. It was Patrick, followed by two tall policemen. One flashed a badge.

Ignoring him, Mark asked Patrick, "Have you seen Maggie?"

Patrick nodded. "I just talked to Dr. Braverman. He says she's got a good chance. Maggie's strong, but they won't know anything until she comes out of surgery."

The officer shouldered his way in front of Patrick. "Mr. Wilde, I'll need a statement."

A young woman wearing a stethoscope around her neck barged over and looked Mark up and down. "Do you want to take it now, officer, or can I see to this man first? He's bleeding and I think he'll need some stitches. That head wound looks pretty ragged."

Dr. Zachery guided Mark to the emergency room, made him sit on a gurney, and drew a curtain halfway around the high, narrow bed. She unbuttoned what was left of his shirt and dropped it on the floor.

"Close call, I'd say. Another half inch and you'd be in surgery." The bullet had creased down his back, taking the top two layers of skin with it. Some particularly nasty scrapes and bruises on his shoulders were dark with blood.

Mark didn't respond, just gritted his teeth when the doctor applied antiseptic.

"You've got a nasty cut on your head. I'll need to take a few stitches, get some X-rays."

"What for?" Mark growled.

"We always take X-rays when head injuries are involved," she said patiently. "And I'd like you to stay in the hospital tonight. Unless I miss my guess, you've got a dandy concussion. I'll give you something for the pain."

Mark shook his head.

"Oh, I see," the doctor drawled sarcastically. "The strong, silent, macho type. Well, a couple of hours from now you may change your tune.

You're in shock, but when it wears off, you're going to feel pretty awful.''

Not as bad as Maggie, he said to himself. *And it's my fault.* If he hadn't grabbed the gun from Rawnick, she wouldn't have taken the hit. He'd charged in like a bull in a porcelain factory, and now she was paying the price. A steep one.

One of the policemen ducked his head in. ''We'd like that statement now.''

''You'll have to watch me practice my crosss-titching,'' Dr. Zachery announced in a cheerful voice. ''But do come in.'' She reached for a hypodermic. ''I'm going to give you a shot to numb the area before I sew you up.''

Mark didn't think he could feel any more numb than he already did. The only thing on his mind was Maggie.

The sergeant walked in, clipboard in hand. ''I understand you came on the scene when a man attempted to take Ms. Macguire hostage?''

''Yeah. I came in at the wrong time. I didn't know he had a gun. I just saw his hands on her, hurting her, and I reacted.'' Mark closed his eyes, then opened them again, grimacing at the tugging sensation where his flesh was being sewn together.

He told the officer everything he knew, what he'd found when conducting his investigation, the steps he'd taken to find Rawnick. It wasn't very much.

The officer tipped his hat back. "Rawnick's refusing to talk. He's waiting for the court to appoint a lawyer, but judging from Mr. Macguire's story, it's a pretty good guess he was out for revenge." His eyes narrowed to slits. "And you say you found evidence on the river linking him to a firearm?"

"I found a lighter, inscribed with his name and birth date, in the same place where I found some animals shot with a small-caliber pistol."

"Could be the twenty-two he carried. We've run a check on the piece. It's registered, but we'll get him on attempted kidnapping and assault with a deadly weapon. He'll do time." The officer ran his finger down the clipboard. "That's all I need for now. Where can I find you for the next twenty-four hours?"

Mark gave him a grim look. "Right here."

The officer nodded, then left.

Dr. Zachery shone a penlight in one of his eyes, then the other. "I'm going to check you in for the night."

Mark shook his head. "I don't think so, doc. Just tell me where Maggie is."

"Take the bed," Dr. Zachery insisted. "I'll check on Ms. Macguire and give you a firsthand report."

Mark gave her a bleak look that said he wouldn't go for it.

She shrugged her shoulders. "Have it your way." Retrieving a pad from her pocket, she wrote out a prescription. "Here." She ripped off the sheet of paper. "Get this filled at the hospital pharmacy. It won't knock you out, but you'll feel a lot better in the morning."

He took the paper, folded it, and put it in his jeans pocket. "Uh, doc. . . . " He looked at his ripped and bloodied shirt lying on the floor. "Is there something I can put on?"

Dr. Zachery pulled open a drawer, found the top half of a doctor's green scrubs, and handed it to him.

Mark eased it over one arm, then the other, wincing at the pain in his back. He didn't fill the prescription. He went to the nurses' station and learned Maggie was still in surgery. He made his way to the waiting room. The clock on the wall read after midnight. No one was there except himself.

Pouring a cup of coffee, he wondered what had happened to Patrick. Maybe the doctors had let him see Maggie. Patrick was family. He wasn't. But not for long. If he had his way, that would change. Everything was different now. For tonight, he could only wait and believe that she'd be all right. If she didn't come out of this, he'd break into the local jail and tear Rawnick limb from limb.

He went over it again for the thirtieth time in the last few hours. Why hadn't he waited a split second longer before jumping Rawnick? What if he'd talked him into putting the gun down? Or pointing it at him instead of Maggie? But when he'd seen Rawnick with his burly arm wrapped around her, something had snapped. He could no more have stopped himself from trying to save Maggie than he could stop himself from loving her.

He downed the scalding, bitter coffee, crumpled the paper cup into a ball, and threw it across the room. The pain in his back made him wince. His head ached. He had to stay awake. He had to be there when she came out of surgery.

Patrick came running in. His face looked stricken.

Mark stood up, the chair toppling over behind him. "Is it Maggie?" he asked, his voice broken and hoarse. "Tell me what's happened!"

Chapter Nine

" I don't have any news about Maggie," Patrick told him. "She's still in surgery." He saw the bandage on Mark's head, the wrinkled green smock. "Are you all right?"

Mark shook his head. "Don't worry about me. I'm fine."

Patrick ran a hand over his face. "I just called Kerry. She says the baby's coming."

"Now? You can't be serious," Mark blurted, genuinely astonished.

Patrick nodded his head furiously. "She's been in labor for hours already. She's been with Evelyn all this time, trying to find me. I'm going home to get her now. When I get back, I'll check in." He turned for the door. "Take care of Maggie."

Mark looked up, closed his eyes, and said a silent prayer. If Maggie lived, he'd take care of her from now until eternity. If only he got the chance.

The night wore on. People came and went, waiting for patients being stitched up or bandaged in the emergency room. The sounds of children's cries pierced the air. He didn't know time could pass so slowly. Patrick had run in once to tell him they were admitting Kerry to the maternity ward on the fifth floor. Mark continued to pace back and forth in the waiting room on the first.

A doctor wearing scrubs walked in. He had a serious look to him. Pulling his surgeon's cap off his steel-gray hair, he raked his fingers through it, then glanced around the room.

Mark stood up.

"Mr. Macguire?" The doctor walked over and extended his hand. "Dr. Braverman."

"How is she?" Mark asked without hesitation. If he had to lie about his identity, he would. Patrick had asked him to take care of her, and they wouldn't tell him anything if he wasn't family.

"She's out of surgery. The bullet missed all the vital organs. She's a lucky lady. Three broken ribs, severe contusions to both lungs." The doctor folded his arms across his chest. "She took a severe blow to the head. We won't know the full extent of the concussion until after we run tests."

Mark closed his eyes, then opened them. "Tests?"

"We'll run a CAT scan tomorrow, after she's gained some strength."

"What kind of test is that?"

"Nothing for you to worry about," Dr. Braverman said. "It's an X-ray of the brain. Just to confirm what we suspect—that there's no permanent damage."

The words echoed in Mark's head. Permanent damage. "Can I see her?" he asked, his voice catching in his throat.

"She won't know you," the doctor explained. "She's heavily sedated."

Mark grabbed his arm. "I have to see her now," he insisted, knowing if he didn't, he would go mad.

The doctor looked down at his arm, then up at Mark. "All right. Just for a minute."

Mark didn't know what was worse: all the hours of waiting or seeing her lying there, deathly pale except for the dark bruises shadowing her right temple and along one arm, the tubes hooking her to machines, pumping fluids into her veins.

He moved closer and picked up her hand. It was cool, but he could feel the pulse. It beat softly, telling him she was alive. She wore a white hospital gown. Her skin looked almost as pale.

He kept thinking about it. The instant that had changed their lives. After Henderson told him about the disastrous meeting with Bingham, he'd gone back and asked the director to reconsider his decision. Although he'd reviewed the file again, looking for hard evidence against Rawnick, Bingham had announced his decision was final.

Without missing a heartbeat, Mark had resigned. He couldn't deal with the kind of bureaucracy and regulations that would revoke an outfitter's permit when all the evidence pointed to someone else. He wanted to do more important things with his life. He'd take the offer from the coalition and try to make a real difference. Contribute something important.

After cleaning out his desk and saying good-bye to friends, he'd driven to Sycamore Springs. He wanted to sort things out with Maggie. Tell her he loved her. As he drove through town on his way to her house, he'd noticed the lights on at Outdoor Odyssey.

He'd suspected something was wrong when he heard noises coming from the shed. If only he'd waited an instant longer, until after Rawnick had opened that door, maybe he could have wrestled the gun away before Maggie took the bullet. Before she was thrown to the floor. Before she bounced her head off the old cast-iron wheelbarrow standing in one corner.

He kept his hand on hers through the bars raised on both sides of the hospital bed. A glass wall faced him, and he thought how much Maggie would hate not having a window, not seeing the sky or the tall pine trees standing guard outside the hospital.

She was so pale. *Please God, let her be all right.*

He watched the drip, drip of the liquid running from the bottle, down a tube, and into a needle inserted in her vein. A wooden board taped to her arm prevented her from bending it. He heard a noise and looked up. A nurse tapped on the glass wall, motioning for him to come out. He bent down and touched his lips to her forehead.

''I told them I was your brother so they'd let me see you,'' he whispered. ''They won't let me stay.'' He ran a finger over his lips, then moved it to her mouth, planting his kiss there. ''I'll be hanging around till you're better, sweetheart. Make it soon.'' He let go of her hand and slowly backed out of the room.

He sat in the waiting room for the rest of the night, alternately staring at the clock and pestering the nurses for any change in her condition. They let him see her every hour. He sat by the side of the bed holding her hand until they made him leave, then he calmly returned to the waiting room and watched the dark sky soften into pale sunrise through the plate-glass window.

Dr. Zachery walked into the waiting room, her

mouth set in a thin line. "I checked on you, Mr. Wilde. You didn't have the prescription filled."

"Didn't need it," he told her stiffly.

"Or have the X-rays taken."

He glared at her.

"How do you feel?"

He ran a hand over his chin. The one-day stubble felt stiff. "Got a headache."

"Nurse," Dr. Zachery called over her shoulder, "give me three aspirin and some water, please. How about letting me check those stitches?" She handed him the aspirin and water.

Mark waved her away, but he accepted the white tablets, gulping them down in one swallow.

Dr. Zachery gave him a cynical look. "I hear your 'sister' is doing better."

Mark blinked. The long night without sleep had begun to take its toll. That and the pain. He took a deep breath. The tone of her voice told him she had caught on. "It's the only way they'll let me see her."

"If you agree to the X-ray, I'll add your name to the list of family members."

He met her gaze. "I didn't know doctors made deals," he said, then ran his hand around his neck. He was too tired to think, and he didn't have any other choice. If the doctor reported his true identity, he wouldn't be allowed to see Maggie.

"I'm about to go off duty," Dr. Zachery told

him. "See her first, then I'll take you down to X-ray."

"All right," he agreed, wincing as he got up and headed for intensive care.

Maggie tried to open her eyes. She kept hearing voices and her name being called over and over. She didn't know where she was, but she wasn't in control of her body. She tried to move her hand and nothing happened.

Then she remembered. The single light bulb casting a dull glow around the cluttered storeroom. Patrick, the imprint of fear branded on his face like a tattoo, forced to stand helpless while a gun stabbed her ribs. The sharp blast of the bullet exploding as it left the barrel of the gun. Had she screamed? She'd been pushed, or she'd fallen to the floor. She remembered hitting her head on something sharp and unyielding. Nothing more.

There was something else too. Not reality, almost a dream. Mark had been there—standing over her, then cradling her in his arms. His face looked haggard. He had blood on his head. She heard the voices again. Calling her. Her eyes slit a fraction. People in white, moving around a room with even whiter walls. Harsh fluorescent lights. No sun. No windows. The air smelled stale. Drugs clouded her mind.

She opened her eyes and felt a gentle touch on

her hand. She looked around. Mark. His face was drawn, stubble dotting his chin like tiny brown pinpricks. She tried to say his name, but the only sound she heard was a hoarse croaking. Then the blackness surrounded her again. Strangers lapsed in and out of view, their voices odd and impersonal. They put her on a gurney. When they moved her, the pain in her chest made her cry out. They took her to a room. A huge piece of machinery that looked like some kind of steel monster swallowed her up, gurney and all, and she remembered clicking sounds, like a camera.

She lost all track of time. The mist she struggled to see through became a light haze, and she recognized voices. Patrick. A woman with a deep, soothing voice who wore a doctor's white coat and a stethoscope draped around her neck.

A wave of panic cut through the fog. She saw a bar in front of her. Trapped. Had to get out. "No . . . no!" She flailed her arms in the air. The needle in her arm jerked free, drops of blood splattering the white sheets. Someone held her down and wouldn't let her up.

"Calm down," the woman in the white coat coaxed. "Get Mr. Wilde," she told an orderly. "Stat! He's the only one she responds to."

The doctor turned back to Maggie. "You're in a hospital," she explained. "You've been hurt, but you're going to be all right."

Maggie opened her mouth to talk, then closed it again. She had a compelling desire to close her eyes, to sleep. She resisted it, opened her eyes, and saw a man sitting on a chair next to her. He held her hand in his. "Mark?"

"Yes, sweetheart." He leaned toward her, relief easing the strained expression on his face. "I'm here, baby. I'm here."

She turned her head so she could look at him. Then she remembered. "Is Patrick all right?"

"He's fine."

"They're giving me something. I don't want to sleep anymore."

Mark looked at Dr. Zachery.

"We can try decreasing the dosage," she said.

"I don't want it," Maggie said in a halting voice. The pain started to come back and she steeled herself to fight it. The pain told her she was alive.

The doctor leaned down close. "You'll have to lie still. You had a bullet in your chest and you broke three ribs. If you move around, the tissue surrounding the wounds will tear. We can't do much for broken ribs except keep you immobile."

Maggie nodded, the sweat breaking out on her forehead. "Don't want to sleep," she whispered in a halting voice.

"I'll stay with her," Mark told Dr. Zachery.

The doctor smiled. "Just as you have for the past two days, Mr. Wilde?"

Maggie gasped. "Two days?"

She tried to sit up, but the pain forced her back down.

"Patrick's fine. Rawnick's in jail," Mark told her in a rush, gently massaging her hand.

She slid her eyes over him. "You don't look fine," she said, slowly noticing the haggard look on his face, the bandage covering one eyebrow and a corner of his dark hair.

Mark smiled. "Now that you're awake, I'm more than fine. You gave us a scare."

Dr. Zachery picked up her arm, but she tried to pull it back.

"Ms. Macguire, I have to reinsert the needle into your vein. I'll be as gentle as possible, but it'll help if you lie still."

Maggie winced at the jab, then forced herself to relax. Her head and her chest hurt, and now her arm.

When the doctor finished, Mark expelled his breath in a big whoosh. He picked up Maggie's hand and held it tight.

She had a sudden flash of memory. Mark must have stopped Rawnick. If he hadn't been there, she would have been history, kaput, dead. She'd tried to get away, but Rawnick had been too strong. She looked at Mark, her eyes terrified. "You saved me from that hideous man."

"It's all over now," he reassured her. "You're going to be all right."

A shudder ran through her. She would never know what Rawnick had planned to do to her. Didn't want to. Inching her hand across the bed, she found his and looked up at him.

"Is Rawnick in jail?"

Mark nodded sharply. "For a long time. Not only for what he did to you, but for all the harm he caused Rapid Shooters. The police matched his gun with slugs from the carcasses I brought in from the river, and he admitted that Patrick gave him a list of company rules, including the one prohibiting firearms."

Maggie took a deep breath. "Thank God."

Mark squeezed her hand gently. "Bingham looked at the evidence and decided that Patrick followed every BLM regulation right from the beginning. Rawnick was the one who broke the rules *and* the law. Your permit has been reinstated and you're back in business."

"You've taken care of everything," she whispered softly, then realized how exhausted he looked. He had a rough, three-day stubble, and his eyes were haggard, lined with deep circles.

"Where've you been sleeping?" she asked.

"There's a couple of cots down the hall for

interns. I bunk down for a few hours now and then.''

"Nice shirt." she commented dryly, noticing the material stretched tightly across his chest. The buttons puckered and looked as if they might pop. ''Patrick's?''

He grinned, embarrassed. ''I've been showering and changing at your house.''

"Where is he?'' She wanted to see her brother, make sure he was all right.

Mark knew he'd have to tell her. She would get excited again, come unglued, and he knew that too. But he didn't want to keep anything from her ever again. He'd learned a lesson. He'd almost lost her twice—once because of a stupid lie and the second time because of a criminal. There wouldn't be a third. He loved her. He only had to convince her that they could make it work. Marriage, babies. The whole shebang. ''Patrick's here in the hospital.''

She looked at him with frightened eyes. ''But you said he wasn't hurt.''

"He isn't. The night you were shot, Kerry went into labor—''

Maggie's eyes widened, her face paling even whiter. ''Is she all right? The baby?''

"They're fine.'' A slow smile creased his face. ''You have a new niece.''

"A girl?'' A smile spread across her face, then

she sighed. "A girl." She gripped Mark's hand. "I want to see her."

"You're not supposed to get up."

"I don't care."

"Maggie, the doctor—"

Her lips clamped down hard and a flush reddened her complexion. "I don't give a hoot what the doctor says. Either you get me over to see my niece and my sister-in-law, or I'll get there by myself."

"You're better, all right," Mark said, cocking his head to one side. "You've got that stubborn look on your pretty face."

"No stalling," she said. "Are you taking me, or am I calling a cab?"

A mischievous look settled over his features. "How about a ride in a wheelchair, milady?"

"Can you get one?"

"Are you kidding?" He threw out both arms. "You want the moon? No problem. The stars?" He swept one arm through the air. "You've got it. A wheelchair's a piece of cake."

She breathed easier and smiled when he left the room. She couldn't ask for a sweeter guy. And he obviously intended to treat her like royalty.

Mark returned a minute later, pushing a wheelchair in front of him. "Your wish is my command. The very latest, four-wheel-drive, stainless-steel model."

After carefully settling Maggie in the leather seat, he put the intravenous bottle in a holder attached to the wheelchair, grabbed a blanket from the bed, and tucked it around her.

"Ready?"

She bit down hard on her lip and gripped the narrow arms of the chair. The pain passed.

"Maggie, are you all right?" He bent down by her side. He couldn't stand to see her in pain. He wanted to take care of her, now and forever.

"Yes," she assured him. "Just a minute." She tried to raise an unsteady hand to her hair.

"Here, let me." He pulled a wide-toothed comb out of his back pocket and attempted to smooth out the tangles. He angled his head this way and that, then combed her hair again. Taking a step back, he gave a long, low wolf whistle. "Gorgeous. Simply gorgeous."

She rolled her eyes. "In a gnat's eye, but thanks for trying. Come on. The baby's two days old and I haven't seen her yet."

Mark checked the hallway in both directions, then steered her toward the door. "It's all clear. Let's go while the getting's good."

The elevator doors opened and Maggie got her first glimpse of the maternity ward. There were rainbows and puffy white clouds painted on blue walls. As they passed the nurses' station, she glanced at the photos of the newborn babies taped to the glass wall. This wing of the hospital was filled with families, husbands and wives, babies just beginning their lives. She had come close to losing hers.

"Here we are," Mark announced, opening the wide door and wheeling her in.

Maggie took in the bright patchwork quilt at the foot of the bed, the beribboned bassinet, and the padded rocking chair positioned on one side of the room. A comfortable couch stood against the other wall. Kerry had told her about the birthing suite, but this was like something out of a book. She'd been away too long and seen too many babies born in huts in the jungle.

"Maggie!" Patrick and Kerry called out at the same time.

"She wouldn't wait," Mark explained. "She was afraid that baby girl wouldn't know her aunt if another minute passed."

Kerry scrambled out of bed with Patrick at her side, and went over to Maggie. "How're you feeling? Are you all right?"

"I'm fine . . . fine." She took Kerry's hand. "Shouldn't you be resting?"

Kerry's grin was as bright as sunshine. "Goodness, no. I'm a new mother, not an invalid. Do you want to hold the baby?"

Maggie grinned back. "Please."

Patrick went to the bassinet and returned with

a bundle wrapped in pink and white. "Here she is," he announced, leaning down and easing his daughter into Maggie's arms. "We've named her Elizabeth Margaret."

Maggie's quick intake of breath mirrored the feeling that warmed her heart. She blinked back the tears. "Elizabeth Margaret," she whispered.

"After Mother and you," Patrick explained. "Those we love most. We've lost one, and you. . . . " He shook his head. "Too close a call."

"Oh, Patrick." She looked at him, her eyes misty. When Maggie gently moved the blanket away from the tiny face, her breath caught. The curls covering the baby's head like a silky, golden cap were the same shade as her own.

"Red, like yours," Mark said, bending down next to Maggie. "Curls and all."

Maggie gently pressed a finger against Elizabeth Margaret's hand and watched the tiny fingers wrap around hers. Then the baby opened her eyes. They were an incredible shade of pale blue. Maggie finally managed to breathe. "She's perfect," she said, watching the baby wrinkle up her face and make cooing noises.

"Mark nicknamed her Lizbeth the first time he held her," Patrick said.

Maggie looked up at Mark. "You've held the baby?"

Kerry's cheery laugh echoed around the room. "A dozen times."

Mark took the baby from Maggie, cradling her in his arms. "Lizbeth and I have become very good friends, haven't we, sweetheart?" he said softly, brushing his lips across the baby's cheek.

Maggie couldn't believe her eyes. Mark's face was positively glowing, and he was making little cooing sounds at the baby! What was going on? It was remarkable, watching this big, powerful man handle such a small newborn package with such tenderness and love.

Maggie looked at Lizbeth, then back to Mark. The smile on his face said everything. His eyes were as bright as the sun shining through the window. He seemed as happy and proud of the newest Macguire as Lizbeth's parents were. She didn't know what had happened in the last few days, but she was sorry she'd missed it.

Maggie saw the happiness and contentment that filled Kerry's eyes, and she saw the same look on her brother's face as Mark settled Lizbeth in Kerry's arms.

"It's a miracle, seeing your first child born," Patrick said. "But it's a little scary too."

Maggie heard Mark let out a sigh, then say, "I can hardly wait to have kids."

Glancing up at him, she was caught off guard by the soft look in his dark eyes, the tender expression she read on his face. Remembering his earlier hesitation at the thought of children, she was stunned.

He looked down at her, their eyes meeting, their attention caught up in each other. "I never had a real family and I want to be there for my kids. Teaching them to play football, going fishing, backpacking in the wilderness, learning how to tie knots." He smiled and looked over at Patrick. "You know, I always wanted to be a Boy Scout—"

Patrick just laughed. "And what if you have a half dozen girls?"

Mark screwed up his mouth. "I don't see any difference. Maggie won't spend much time cooking and cleaning."

The blood siphoned from her face. "Wait a—"

He bent down next to her, lightly touched her hair, then ran his fingers through the messy curls. "No," he whispered. "Let's not wait. I don't want to."

Maggie stared at him wordlessly. She never would have believed Mark would share her vision of a family. The one her parents had given her. And when she saw the way Mark was with Lizbeth, there was a tug at her heart she'd never felt before and couldn't explain.

"We've asked Mark to be godfather," Patrick announced solemnly. "Dad would've liked that.

Mark saved your life. He's part of the family now.''

Mark leaned over and brushed his lips across Maggie's forehead, then one cheek. ''I'm not part of the family until this woman promises to marry me.''

Maggie blinked. ''I don't think this is the time—''

''This is the perfect time, sweetheart,'' he said. ''I almost lost you. I can't wait any longer.'' His voice lowered and he took one of her hands in his. ''I love you. I have since the day I first saw you.'' He closed his eyes for an instant, then pressed her hand to his lips.

''I love you too,'' she whispered breathlessly.

''And you'll marry me?''

She laughed. ''Can you wait until I'm out of this wheelchair?''

He bent down next to her and brushed his lips across hers. ''If I have to, sweetheart. Only if I have to.''

DATE DUE

JAN 2 8			
APR 1 2 1994			
GAYLORD			PRINTED IN U.S.A.